AM I DEPRESSED?

THE STRUGGLE FOR LIGHT IN A DARKENED WORLD

TARUN MAJUMDER

Contents

Contents

Foreword

In a world that constantly demands more from us, it's easy to lose ourselves. The pursuit of success, the pressure of expectations, and the quiet weight of societal norms can slowly erode our sense of well-being. For many, this internal battle becomes too heavy to ignore, yet it remains one of the most misunderstood struggles of our time. Am I Depressed? is not just a question—it's an exploration, an invitation to examine the complexity of our emotional landscape.

This book takes us into the life of Asmita, a 30-year-old woman who is grappling with the deep, often invisible forces of depression. Through her journey, we see the transformation of a person who once thrived under the pressures of life into someone who is confronting her own internal darkness. But beyond the sadness and confusion, Asmita's story is one of self-discovery, courage, and healing. She is not defined by her depression, but shaped by the way she chooses to confront it.

What makes Am I Depressed? unique is its raw authenticity. It doesn't provide easy answers or romanticize mental illness; rather, it presents depression as it truly is—complex, unpredictable, and deeply personal. But within that complexity, there is hope. There is strength in vulnerability, and there is power in asking for help when we need it.

In reading this book, we are reminded that depression is not something to be ashamed of. It is not a flaw or weakness but a part of the human experience. For those who have struggled with their mental health, Asmita's journey will feel familiar. For those who have not, this book offers a window into the reality that millions of people face every day. It calls us to be more compassionate, more understanding, and more open to the conversations that have long been silenced.

As you read Am I Depressed?, I encourage you to reflect on the complexities of mental health and the importance of asking questions, even when the answers are difficult to find. Depression, like all mental health challenges, is a journey—one that requires empathy, patience, and the willingness to seek support. Asmita's story is a reminder that even in the darkest moments, we are never truly alone.

This book is not just for those who are struggling with depression; it is for anyone who has ever questioned their emotional well-being or wondered how to support a loved one through their own challenges. It is an invitation to explore, to learn, and to grow. It is a testament to the power of self-awareness, the resilience of the human spirit, and the healing that can come from simply being seen and understood.

ONE

THE MIDNIGHT CALL

The clock on Asmita's nightstand flickered, casting faint shadows across the dim room. It was 3:15 AM. She rolled over, staring at the ceiling, feeling the weight of the night pressing down on her. Sleep felt like an impossible luxury. Her mind raced, an unrelenting cycle of negative thoughts, each more painful than the last. She closed her eyes tightly, as though to shut them out, but they refused to go away.

Her phone sat on the bedside table, glowing faintly in the darkness. She picked it up, her thumb hovering over the screen for a moment. It was stupid, calling someone at this hour. But then, she couldn't stand it anymore. The silence, the isolation, the thoughts... they were too much.

With a shaky breath, she dialed the number.

Sangeeta's phone rang. She was sound asleep, curled up in the warmth of her blanket, the peaceful hum of the city outside her window barely audible. But the ring cut through the stillness like a knife. Groggily, she reached for her phone, squinting at the screen. It was Asmita. At 3:15 AM.

Sangeeta answered on the second ring, her voice laced with confusion and concern. "Asmita? Is everything okay?"

On the other end, Asmita's voice was fragile, almost breaking under the weight of the words she couldn't hold inside any longer. "I... I can't sleep, Sangeeta. I don't know what's happening to me."

Sangeeta sat up, rubbing her eyes to shake off the remnants of sleep. "What do you mean? What's going on? Talk to me."

Asmita sniffed, trying to hold back the tears that threatened to spill. "I just... feel like I'm suffocating. All these horrible thoughts keep swirling around in my head. I don't know what to do with them. It's like they're taking over, and I can't stop them."

Sangeeta felt her heart tighten, the deep bond of friendship making her instantly alert. "Hey, it's okay. You're not alone. I'm right here. Let's take it slow. What are these thoughts, Asmita? Can you tell me?"

Asmita paused for a long moment, the silence on the line heavy with her emotions. "It's like... I'm failing at everything. My job, my life, just everything. And no matter how hard I try, nothing gets better. I feel like I'm just drifting... and I don't know how to snap out of it. I don't know who I am anymore."

Sangeeta's voice softened, but there was a strength in it now. "Asmita, listen to me. You are not a failure. I know it doesn't feel like it right now, but I've known you for years, and you are one of the strongest people I know. Don't let these thoughts convince you otherwise."

"I don't feel strong," Asmita whispered, her voice breaking. "I feel... so small. So insignificant."

Sangeeta leaned back against the headboard, her mind racing, searching for the right words. "You're not small.

You're not insignificant. I know it's hard to see that right now, but you are loved. You are important, and this moment—this feeling—it's temporary. But I'm always here for you, okay? You don't have to face this alone."

Asmita exhaled shakily, the tears she'd been holding back finally falling. "What if I can't get out of this? What if it never ends?"

Sangeeta stayed silent for a moment, allowing the weight of Asmita's words to settle. Then, gently, she replied, "You will get through this. It might not happen overnight, but you will get through it. And when you're ready, we'll figure out what comes next together."

"I don't even know where to start," Asmita murmured.

"You don't have to have all the answers right now," Sangeeta reassured her. "One step at a time. Maybe the first step is just talking about it. And you're doing that now."

Asmita wiped her face with the back of her hand, her breathing still uneven but starting to calm. "I don't know how to thank you, Sangeeta. I feel so broken, and I hate it."

Sangeeta's voice was soft but firm. "You're not broken, Asmita. You're human. And humans have moments like this. We all do. Don't let this define you. Let's take it one day at a time, okay? You've got me, always."

Asmita sniffed, a fragile smile tugging at the corner of her lips. "One day at a time. Yeah, okay."

The silence that followed was quieter now, less suffocating. Asmita could feel the weight lifting, even if just a little. Sangeeta's words, her presence, even through the phone, were the anchors she had needed.

"Thanks, Sangeeta," Asmita whispered. "I'll try. I promise."

"Whenever you need to talk, I'm just a call away," Sangeeta replied, her voice soothing. "We'll get through this, okay?"

Asmita nodded even though she knew Sangeeta couldn't see it. "Okay. Goodnight, Sangeeta."

"Goodnight, Asmita. Sleep well. I'm here."

The line clicked off, and Asmita lay there in the quiet, her heart still racing but her mind just a little bit lighter. She didn't have all the answers. But for the first time in what felt like forever, she knew she wasn't alone in this fight.

TWO

THE UNSETTLING NIGHT

Sangeeta tossed and turned in bed, her mind restless despite the late hour. The weight of the conversation with Asmita lingered in her thoughts, gnawing at her insides. She kept replaying Asmita's words over and over: "I feel so small. So insignificant. I don't know how to fix it." Those words were still echoing in Sangeeta's head, keeping her wide awake long after they'd ended their call. It was the silence that worried her—the silence between the lines, the things Asmita hadn't said.

Sangeeta glanced at the clock beside her bed. It was 4:30 AM now, and she still couldn't shake the feeling that something wasn't right. Asmita's struggle, the rawness in her voice, felt more than just sleeplessness. Sangeeta couldn't help but wonder—was it more than just depression? What if Asmita's symptoms were leaning toward something even darker, something like manic depression? What if she was on the edge, not just struggling with isolation but teetering on the brink of making a dangerous choice?

The thought chilled Sangeeta. She knew the signs, had heard the stories, and the last thing she wanted was for Asmita to slip into that place of despair where the darkness consumed everything. She couldn't let that happen. Not on her watch.

Sitting up in bed, Sangeeta tried to push the worry aside, but it wouldn't budge. What if Asmita needed her now, more than ever? What if the night turned worse, and by morning, it was too late?

Sangeeta grabbed her phone, her fingers hovering over the screen, and then, in a burst of urgency, she dialed Asmita's number again. The phone rang, and Sangeeta held her breath, praying Asmita would pick up. The call connected, and after a few moments, Asmita's tired voice answered.

"Hello?" Asmita's voice was weaker than before, but there was an edge of something like relief in it.

"Sangeeta, why are you calling again? Is everything okay?" Asmita asked, clearly surprised.

"Hey, I couldn't sleep either," Sangeeta replied, trying to sound casual, though the knot in her stomach wouldn't loosen. "Just wanted to check in, make sure you're okay."

Asmita let out a soft, tired chuckle. "I'm fine. Just trying to get through the night, you know? Not much else to do."

Sangeeta's mind raced as she tried to keep her tone light. "I get that. I know it's hard, especially when the night drags on. Sometimes, our minds just race, and it's hard to quiet them down."

A silence stretched between them, and Sangeeta could hear the faint sounds of Asmita's breathing, heavier now, as if she was sinking deeper into her thoughts. Sangeeta pressed on, knowing she had to keep Asmita talking, keep her from retreating into that darkness alone.

"Hey, you've been through a lot lately, right?" Sangeeta began, carefully picking her words. "I know things have been rough with your break-up. Do you want to talk about it?"

Asmita hesitated before answering, her voice tinged with sadness. "I don't really want to think about it, but... I guess it's part of the reason I'm up right now. It still hurts. It feels like everything's falling apart. I thought I'd be fine, but... maybe I wasn't ready for it."

"I get it," Sangeeta said, her voice soft but firm. "Break-ups are never easy, and it's okay to still feel the pain. But you're not alone in this, Asmita. You've got me."

Asmita sighed, the sound thick with emotion. "I don't know, Sangeeta. I feel so... out of control. I'm not even sure who I am anymore."

Sangeeta's heart sank. This wasn't just about the break-up. There was more to it, much more. "Listen, Asmita," Sangeeta said, her voice gentle but insistent. "I know things feel really heavy right now, and it's okay to feel lost. But you don't have to carry this alone. I know someone—her name is Paromita. She's a really good psychologist, a childhood friend of mine. She's helped a lot of people, and I think it might be a good idea to talk to her. She could help you figure out what's going on, what you're really feeling."

Asmita was silent for a long time, and Sangeeta could feel the weight of the silence press against her. Finally, Asmita spoke, her voice small but steady.

"I'm not crazy, Sangeeta," she said, almost in a whisper. "I'm not going to do anything drastic, I promise. I'm not thinking about... ending things, or something like that. I swear."

Sangeeta felt a wave of relief wash over her, but it was tempered with worry. "I know you're not crazy, Asmita," she replied, her voice thick with emotion. "You're just going through something really hard right now, and it's okay to ask for help. It's okay to need it. And I want you to know that you don't have to face this by yourself. I'll be with you every step of the way."

Asmita let out a shaky breath. "I'm scared, Sangeeta. Scared that I'll never feel better. Scared that I'll always feel like this."

Sangeeta's heart broke for her. "I understand. But I promise you, this isn't forever. Things will get better. It might take time, and it might not be easy, but you're not alone. And you don't have to do it all by yourself. Let me help you find the right path."

There was a long pause, and when Asmita spoke again, her voice was quieter, but there was a sense of resolve in it. "Okay. I'll think about it. Maybe I'll meet with Paromita. But not yet. I'm not ready to make that leap. But... I'm glad you're here. I don't think I could do this without you."

Sangeeta smiled softly, her chest heavy with both relief and concern. "You don't have to do it alone, Asmita. I'm not going anywhere. I'll stay on the phone with you until the morning if I have to. We'll get through this together."

Asmita's voice was barely a whisper when she finally spoke again. "Thanks, Sangeeta. For everything."

Sangeeta sat back against her pillows, the weight of the night settling around her. The darkness outside mirrored the heaviness in her heart, but she wouldn't leave Asmita alone in it. Not tonight. Not ever.

And so, they talked, until the first light of dawn began to creep through the windows, until the night's silence was broken, and the long, dark hours felt a little less unbearable. Sangeeta knew they weren't out of the woods yet, but for tonight, she had done something. She had made sure

Asmita was not alone. And that, she hoped, was a step toward healing.

THREE

THE MEETING WITH PAROMITA

The soft chime of the café doorbell rang out as Sangeeta stepped inside, the warmth and bustle of the place providing a welcome contrast to the heavy thoughts that had been weighing on her all morning. She spotted Paromita at a corner table, already sitting with a cup of coffee, her glasses perched delicately on her nose as she scanned through some papers. Sangeeta smiled, feeling a bit of relief at seeing her childhood friend again, the familiar face a comfort in the midst of all the uncertainty with Asmita.

Paromita looked up, her eyes lighting up as she saw Sangeeta approach. "Sangeeta! It's so good to see you," she said, standing up to give her a quick hug.

"Likewise," Sangeeta replied, settling into the chair opposite Paromita. "I've been a mess lately."

"I know," Paromita said with a knowing look, her voice steady but warm. "You've been worried about Asmita."

Sangeeta nodded, the worry returning to her chest. "Yeah, I don't know how to help her. She's been struggling so much, and I think it's more than just sadness. I'm scared, Paromita. What if she's on the edge of something more serious?"

Paromita took a slow breath, then set aside her papers. "First, I'm glad you reached out to me. Let's take this one step at a time. It's clear you care deeply about Asmita, and that's the first thing we need when dealing with something like this."

Sangeeta felt a wave of relief, but the knot in her stomach remained. "So... what exactly is happening to her? What are the signs? Could it be something like manic depression?"

Paromita's expression became serious, but there was a calmness in her voice that immediately put Sangeeta at ease. "Okay, let's break this down. Depression can manifest in a lot of different ways, and it doesn't always look the same for everyone. But there are certain early symptoms that we can look for, things that might signal the need for professional help."

She took a sip of her coffee, gathering her thoughts. "In general, depression is more than just feeling sad. It's a prolonged state of emotional numbness or hopelessness. People with depression often lose interest in things they once enjoyed, struggle with energy and motivation, and experience persistent negative thoughts. It's not just a mood shift—it's a pervasive, chronic condition that affects nearly every aspect of a person's life."

Sangeeta listened intently, feeling a sense of dread building in her chest. "So, what could be some of the early symptoms in someone like Asmita?"

"Well," Paromita continued, "it can start with sleep disturbances. Difficulty sleeping, or sleeping too much, is often one of the first signs. Asmita mentioned feeling like she couldn't sleep, which is a classic symptom. Along with that, a sense of deep fatigue, feelings of worthlessness, irritability, and a lack of concentration. Depression often takes away the ability to focus on even the most simple tasks, and over time, this can make someone feel completely overwhelmed and hopeless."

Sangeeta's mind raced as she thought back to their conversations. "That sounds just like her... She keeps saying she feels like she's failing, that nothing is going right."

"Exactly," Paromita replied. "Those are classic signs. And it's important to remember that depression is a medical condition. It's not something someone can just 'snap out of.' It's rooted in biological, psychological, and environmental factors. And when left untreated, it can spiral."

Sangeeta felt a pang of guilt. "I should've seen it sooner. I didn't realize it was this serious."

"You're doing the right thing now, Sangeeta," Paromita said reassuringly. "Recognizing the problem is the first step. The next is getting Asmita the help she needs. That's where therapy and, in some cases, medication can make a real difference."

"How do we know when therapy and medication are necessary?" Sangeeta asked, her brow furrowed in concern. "Couldn't it just be... a phase?"

Paromita shook her head. "It's never just a phase. Depression can't be brushed off as something temporary, especially when it persists for weeks or months. When someone's symptoms interfere with their daily life, relationships, and work, that's when therapy is needed. And in more severe cases, antidepressant medication may be prescribed. It's all about finding the right treatment for the individual."

"That makes sense," Sangeeta said thoughtfully, though the reality of the situation was settling in deeper than ever before. "But what about something like manic depression? Could it be that?"

"Manic depression, or bipolar disorder, is a different condition, though it does overlap with depression in some ways. People with bipolar disorder experience extreme mood swings—periods of intense depression followed by phases of mania or hypomania, where they feel overly energetic, impulsive, and sometimes engage in risky behavior. It's important to distinguish between the two because the treatment for bipolar disorder often involves different medications."

Sangeeta nodded, feeling a bit more informed. "So, how do we know if Asmita's symptoms point to something like that, or if it's just depression?"

"It can be tricky," Paromita said, her expression serious. "What's key here is tracking the symptoms over time. Mania doesn't just happen overnight. If Asmita is showing signs of extreme energy, irritability, or risky behavior, then we'd have to look at bipolar disorder. But from what you've described, I think it's more likely she's experiencing a major depressive episode. Still, the best course of action would be for her to see a professional who can assess her condition in person."

Sangeeta felt a mix of relief and concern. "So, should I suggest therapy to her? I'm scared she'll resist."

"That's a valid concern," Paromita said thoughtfully. "Some people feel a sense of shame or fear about seeing a therapist. They think it means they're weak or 'crazy.' But therapy isn't about that. It's about helping them find a way to cope with and understand their emotions. I'd suggest starting by normalizing the conversation around therapy.

Explain to her that therapy is a safe space, and that it's a step toward taking control of her mental health. And remind her that, just like we see a doctor for physical health, mental health needs care too."

Sangeeta took a deep breath, feeling the weight of the responsibility settle on her shoulders. "I'll talk to her about it. I just don't want to push her too hard, you know?"

"I know," Paromita said. "But trust me, Sangeeta, the fact that you're here, talking about it, already makes you a big part of the solution. Just keep being there for her, and keep the conversation open. We'll find the best way forward."

They sat there for a long while, talking through the history of depression—how it had been understood in earlier times and how current research was constantly evolving. Paromita explained the latest findings in neuroscience and psychology, sharing her insights into how depression affected the brain's chemical balance and what treatments were most effective. They spoke about the stigma that still surrounded mental health, especially in their culture, and how important it was to challenge those misconceptions.

The conversation flowed easily, and as the hours passed, Sangeeta felt a renewed sense of clarity. There was still a long road ahead for Asmita, but now, she had the knowledge and the support to help guide her friend through it.

As the sun began to set, casting a soft golden glow over the café, Sangeeta stood up, feeling lighter than when she'd arrived. "Thank you, Paromita," she said, her voice filled with gratitude. "I can't tell you how much this means."

Paromita smiled, her eyes warm and knowing. "That's what friends are for, Sangeeta. Now, let's make sure Asmita gets the help she deserves."

Sangeeta nodded, feeling more prepared than ever to help her friend face the long, uncertain road ahead. Together, they could find a way through the darkness.

FOUR

"AM I DEPRESSED?"

Asmita sat across from Paromita, her hands clasped tightly together on her lap. She had been silent for a while, the weight of the question hanging in the air, but it was a question that had been swirling in her mind for what felt like an eternity. Finally, she let out a breath and asked, her voice quiet but steady, "Am I depressed?"

Paromita smiled gently, not in a dismissive way, but in a manner that conveyed understanding. "That's the question we're going to explore together, Asmita. And I'm here to listen, so take your time."

Asmita nodded slowly. Her gaze dropped to the floor for a moment before she spoke again. "I don't know how I got here. It started so... small. It was just a phase, I thought. But now... it feels like it's everywhere. I can't shake it. I just want to know, is it depression? Is this what that feels like?"

Paromita leaned forward slightly, her voice calm and reassuring. "It's good that you're asking. Sometimes, just asking the question is the first step toward understanding what's going on. Depression is different for everyone, but it's more than just sadness. It's a medical condition that affects how you feel, think, and even how you function day-to-day."

Asmita looked up, her expression pensive. "So, this... heaviness I feel isn't just me overreacting? It's not just a phase?"

"No, Asmita," Paromita responded gently. "It's not just a phase. Depression is a medical condition, and it's caused by a combination of biological, psychological, and environmental factors. There's nothing wrong with you for feeling the way you do, but it's important to recognize that it's something that can be treated."

Asmita's eyes seemed to darken as she reflected on her own experiences. "I guess it started small... at first, it was just this feeling of being... I don't know, sorry for myself. Self-pity, maybe. I was sad, bored, and everything just felt... pointless. I didn't feel motivated to do anything, didn't want to get out of bed. It was like life had lost its color. But over time, it just... got worse."

Paromita nodded, encouraging her to continue. "Tell me more about how it's been getting worse. How is it affecting you now?"

Asmita hesitated for a moment, as if sorting through the words, before answering, "It's starting to affect my job. I can't focus, I'm making mistakes I shouldn't be making. It's like my mind isn't working the way it used to. And my sleep—it's awful. I either can't fall asleep at all, or I sleep for hours but still feel tired when I wake up. It's like my body is shut down. And then there's my relationships. Even though I've gotten over my break-up, I'm pushing people away. I don't know why, but I just... can't bring myself to care."

Paromita listened attentively, her gaze never leaving Asmita's face. She knew this was the moment of truth, where Asmita was truly starting to open up. "It sounds like depression is really affecting every part of your life, Asmita.

Your job, your sleep, and your relationships. That's exactly why it's important to recognize it for what it is, and not just write it off as something temporary. Depression can seep into every aspect of your life if it's not addressed."

Asmita looked down, wringing her hands nervously. "But the thing is, I feel like I should be over this. My break-up wasn't recent. I've had time to move on. So why am I still like this? Why can't I just... feel better?"

Paromita's voice was soft but firm. "Healing from a break-up—or any other life stress—isn't always linear. Sometimes, it can feel like you've moved past something, but the emotional toll it took on you doesn't always show up right away. And sometimes, it doesn't go away just because we think we've processed it. Depression doesn't always have one clear cause, and it doesn't always resolve when we expect it to. It can be a long-term struggle, and that's okay."

Asmita nodded slowly, but there was a touch of frustration in her eyes. "So... it's not just me being weak?"

Paromita shook her head, her tone filled with certainty. "Absolutely not. You're not weak, Asmita. You're going through something that a lot of people experience, and it's not your fault. Depression is not a sign of weakness. It's a sign that something in your body and mind needs support, and that's what we're here for—to find the right way to support you through this."

A long silence passed between them. Asmita sat back in her chair, feeling the weight of the conversation. There was something comforting in hearing Paromita validate her experience, but it also felt daunting, like she had finally admitted something she had been hiding from herself for too long.

"How do I get out of this?" Asmita asked quietly, her voice barely above a whisper.

"That's what we'll figure out together," Paromita said gently. "We'll take it one step at a time. Therapy can help you work through the thoughts and feelings that are keeping you stuck. And there are other treatment options we can explore if we think they're necessary. But first, I want to continue this conversation, help you understand what's going on, and then we'll decide what the next step is."

Asmita looked up at Paromita, feeling a flicker of hope she hadn't felt in weeks. "Okay," she said, her voice small but filled with a quiet determination. "I'm ready to try."

Paromita gave her a warm, reassuring smile. "That's all we need. Taking the first step is the hardest part, and you've already done that. We'll keep moving forward, one step at a time, and we'll find the right way to help you feel better."

As the session began to wind down, Paromita sat back, her expression thoughtful. She knew that to help Asmita fully understand what was going on inside her, she needed to explain the biological aspect of depression. It wasn't just about thoughts and emotions—it was also about how the body was responding on a deeper, physiological level.

"Asmita," Paromita began, "I think it's important to explain a little more about what's happening in your brain and body during depression. A lot of people don't realize that depression has a scientific basis—it's not just in your head."

Asmita's eyes widened, curious. "You mean there's science behind it?"

"Yes," Paromita said, nodding. "Depression involves chemical changes in the brain, specifically in neurotransmitters—chemicals that transmit signals between nerve cells. Two of the main neurotransmitters involved are serotonin and dopamine, which are often referred to as the 'feel-good' chemicals. When you're depressed, these chemicals are imbalanced, which means your brain isn't processing emotions or signals in the way it should."

She paused to let that sink in before continuing. "On top of that, there are hormonal changes that also play a significant role. For example, cortisol, the hormone that's released when you're stressed, is often elevated in people with depression. This chronic increase in cortisol can lead to fatigue, sleep disturbances, and even cognitive problems—like the difficulty concentrating that you mentioned. It's like your body is in a constant state of heightened stress, which only deepens the depression."

Asmita frowned slightly. "So, it's not just me feeling weak or lazy. My brain is actually... chemically out of balance?"

"Exactly," Paromita replied. "And it's important to understand that these changes are not something you can control on your own. It's not about willpower or just snapping out of it. It's a medical condition that requires treatment. That's why therapy is so important—it helps you address both the emotional and the biological aspects of depression. In some cases, medications can also help to restore the chemical balance in the brain, which can make it easier for you to cope with the emotional and psychological aspects."

Asmita was quiet for a moment, taking it all in. "I never realized how much it affects my body, too."

"It does," Paromita said. "Depression is not just an emotional experience. It's a full-body experience, and that's why we need a comprehensive approach to treatment. We'll work together to find what's best for you—whether that's therapy, medication, or a combination of both."

Asmita nodded slowly, the weight of the information settling in. "I guess I never thought about depression in such a physical way."

Paromita smiled softly. "That's why we're having this conversation. You're not alone in this, Asmita. There's a way through it, and we'll find it, together."

Asmita left the session feeling both overwhelmed and enlightened. The science behind her condition had been an eye-opener, and it helped her understand that her struggles weren't just a reflection of her weakness. It was a complex, physiological issue that could be treated. And for the first time in a long while, she felt a small spark of hope. She was ready to take the next step.

FIVE

Unraveling Ties

It had been a fun night—one of those rare occasions where Asmita let herself relax and enjoy the company of her friends. The party had been thrown by a mutual acquaintance, and for a few hours, everything had felt carefree. Laughter, clinking glasses, and animated conversations filled the room, and Asmita found herself surrounded by people who genuinely appreciated her, including Subrato's friends. She had even found herself talking more with Sangeeta, who had come along, enjoying the freedom of being around familiar faces and, for once, not thinking about anything else.

But now, as they returned to their apartment, the weight of the evening shifted in the air. The bright lights of the apartment seemed too harsh as Asmita walked in, laughing a little too loudly at something Sangeeta had said. She could feel the buzz of the wine still lingering in her veins, a light warmth that had helped her feel more open, more at ease.

But as she glanced over at Subrato, she knew something was off. His posture was stiff, his jaw tight, and his eyes narrowed. He didn't say anything at first, but the silence spoke volumes.

Asmita dropped her purse on the couch and walked over to the kitchen, trying to shake off the unease. "It was a great night," she said, a smile still playing at the corners of her lips. "Everyone loved the dish you made—so many compliments for your cooking." Subrato said, his voice dripping with sarcasm.

He leaned against the doorframe, arms crossed, watching her with an intensity that made Asmita feel self-conscious. "Yeah, I saw that," he said, his words laced with something she couldn't quite place—irritation, maybe? "Some of my friends couldn't stop praising you. I didn't know you were so close with them."

Asmita paused, her smile faltering slightly. "What do you mean? They were just being friendly."

Subrato's eyes flashed with something darker. "Friendly, huh?" he said, his tone sharp. "You seemed pretty comfortable with them. Too comfortable."

Asmita blinked, taken aback by the sudden shift in his mood. "I didn't do anything wrong, Subrato. I was just being myself."

He stepped closer, the space between them closing in a way that made Asmita feel trapped. "Yeah, yourself," he muttered, his voice tight. "But you don't need to be that happy with other people. Especially my friends."

Asmita's chest tightened, her throat constricting as she processed his words. "What are you talking about? We were just talking, enjoying the night. You were with your friends too."

He scoffed, throwing his hands up in frustration. "I don't care about them, Asmita. I care about you. I want you to be happy, but I want you to be happy with me—not with everyone else."

There it was—the first real hint of possessiveness, of control. Asmita's stomach twisted, but she tried to stay calm. "Subrato, I am happy with you," she said quietly. "I'm happy with my friends too, though. I need both. It's not about choosing one over the other."

Subrato's eyes darkened even further. "And another thing," he said, his voice lowering, "I noticed you had a little more to drink than usual tonight."

Asmita felt her face flush. "I wasn't drunk, Subrato. Just a glass more than I usually have."

He scoffed again. "You didn't need to drink at all. I don't like it when you drink. You know that."

She felt a knot tighten in her stomach. "You never said anything before, though. Why now?"

"I don't have to say everything," Subrato snapped, stepping back, his tone harsh. "It's just... you get too carefree, too open when you drink. I don't like it. It's not... who you really are."

Asmita opened her mouth to respond, but the words caught in her throat. His jealousy—his control over her actions, her choices, her friendships—was becoming clearer. She had always known he didn't like her drinking, but she never imagined it would come to this—a silent accusation that her happiness with her friends was somehow a betrayal to him.

"I'm just having a good time, Subrato," Asmita said, her voice steady but filled with frustration. "I'm allowed to enjoy myself, aren't I? Just because I'm happy around my friends doesn't mean I don't care about you. It doesn't mean I don't want to be with you."

Subrato's eyes narrowed. "No, it doesn't mean that. But when you're so happy around them, it makes me feel... unimportant. Like you don't need me anymore. You're mine, Asmita. You should want to be with me, not with anyone else."

Asmita's breath hitched in her chest, a mixture of confusion and discomfort rising within her. She had always felt a sense of possessiveness from him, but tonight, it felt different—darker, more controlling. She tried to steady herself, to find her footing, but the words didn't come easily. "Subrato, that's not fair. I am with you. But I need my space, my friends. You can't expect me to shut them out."

He didn't answer, just stared at her, his gaze cold and unyielding. Asmita felt her heart race as the weight of the situation sank in. This wasn't the man she had first met—the one who had been charming and warm, who had made her feel special and appreciated. This was someone different, someone who wanted to isolate her, control her, and possess her in a way that felt suffocating.

"Maybe you don't understand," Subrato said after a long silence, his voice lower now. "But I don't want to see you happy with anyone else. You belong with me, Asmita. Only me."

The words hung in the air, heavy and final. Asmita stood there, caught in the suffocating silence of his gaze. She had always known he had a possessive side, but this—this was more than she had expected. A part of her felt guilty, but another part of her, the part that still recognized the boundaries of her own identity, bristled at the demand.

She swallowed hard, the weight of the moment pressing down on her chest. "I can't live like this, Subrato," she whispered, almost to herself. "I need to breathe. I need to feel like me again."

He didn't respond, but the hurt in his eyes told her everything she needed to know. Asmita turned away, her heart heavy, the tension between them hanging like a storm cloud, ready to break.

The kitchen still smelled faintly of the dish Asmita had prepared earlier that evening—an intricate chicken curry, slow-cooked with the perfect blend of spices. She had spent hours getting it just right, hoping it would impress Subrato's friends. And it had. Everyone at the party had complimented her on it, and she had been thrilled by the praise, but now, in the silence of their apartment, she could feel the bitterness creeping in.

Subrato's earlier comments about her being "too comfortable" with his friends and her drinking more than usual echoed in her mind. It was clear that his jealousy wasn't just about the wine or the attention from his friends; it was about control. And the more he talked, the more Asmita realized just how far it had gone.

She stood in the kitchen, her back to him, trying to regain her composure. Subrato's footsteps grew louder behind her as he closed the distance, and she could feel the tension in the air thickening.

"Asmita," Subrato said, his voice low, almost controlled, "I just don't get it. You're out there, making everyone think you're perfect. You cooked the perfect dish, smiled, laughed with everyone—except me. I don't feel like I'm a part of your world anymore."

Asmita gripped the counter, her knuckles turning white. "What are you saying? You are part of my world. I'm not pushing you out. But I need more than just you, Subrato. I need my friends, I need my space, and I need to be me."

Subrato's expression tightened as he approached her, his voice rising. "You think you can just have it all? You think you can just play the part of the happy, carefree woman, while I'm stuck here feeling like I'm losing you? You made them love your dish. You impressed them, but what about me, Asmita? What about us?"

The accusation stung, but Asmita didn't back down. She turned to face him, her eyes fierce. "I made them love my dish because I'm proud of what I do, Subrato. And I made you dinner tonight because I wanted to share something with you. But your constant need to control me, to dictate where my attention goes, is suffocating."

Subrato's face flushed, his breathing becoming shallow. He was no longer just angry—he was hurt, and he wasn't hiding it. "It's not about control," he snapped. "I just don't want you to get lost in everyone else. When you're out there with them, it's like I don't even exist. I'm invisible. Why do they matter more than me?"

Asmita took a step back, her heart pounding in her chest. "Because I have a life outside of you, Subrato. A life I can't just erase because it makes you uncomfortable. I don't belong to you."

Subrato's jaw clenched, and he exhaled sharply. "You think you don't belong to me? You think you can be just anyone, do anything, without consequences? You think I'm okay with you laughing with them, enjoying yourself like you did tonight? You think I don't see what's happening here?"

Asmita's breath caught. "What do you mean? What's happening?"

Subrato's voice was low, and there was a dangerous edge to it now. "You're drifting away from me, Asmita. You're becoming someone else. And I'm losing you in the process. The more you smile at your friends, the more I see you being happy with them... the more I feel like I'm losing the person I was supposed to be with. The person I thought was mine."

Her throat constricted as the realization hit her. "Subrato, that's not how relationships work. You don't own me. You don't get to decide who I spend time with or how I act. I am my own person."

His eyes flickered with something—disbelief, anger, maybe both. "You think this is just about them?" he spat, his voice cracking. "This is about you and me. And the way you act around them, the way you act when you're 'free,' makes me feel like I'm nothing. Like I don't matter at all."

Asmita's stomach churned. "What you're describing is control, Subrato. You want me to be yours, and only yours. You want me to shut out everything else—my friends, my happiness, the parts of myself I still hold on to. That's not love. That's possession."

Subrato's face went pale. He stepped back, his voice softening, but the hurt in his eyes was clear. "I'm just afraid. Afraid of losing you. I know you want to be happy with your friends, but what if that happiness is just temporary? What if one day you wake up and realize you don't need me anymore? What if I'm not enough?"

Asmita's breath caught in her throat. "That's not something you get to decide, Subrato. I'm not a possession. I don't belong to you, and I never did. But this—" She gestured between them, the anger still rising in her chest. "This is unhealthy. And I can't keep doing this."

Subrato stood frozen, watching her, a look of disbelief on his face. For a long time, neither of them spoke. The silence in the room was suffocating, thick with the weight of their words. Asmita felt a chill run through her body, her mind racing. The person she had once been with—the man she had once adored—was no longer there. In his place was someone who wanted to define her, shape her into something she didn't recognize.

Finally, after what felt like an eternity, Subrato spoke, his voice quieter now. "So, what do we do now, Asmita? Where do we go from here?"

Asmita closed her eyes for a moment, taking a deep breath. "I don't know, Subrato. But I can't keep pretending that everything is okay when it's not. I need space to figure this out, and I need to be honest with myself. I can't keep sacrificing who I am for this relationship."

His eyes softened, but there was no real apology in them, just a deep sadness. "So, you're saying this is over?"

Asmita felt her heart break just a little, but the truth was clear in her mind. "I don't know what the future holds, but right now, I can't continue like this. Not with you acting this way."

There was a long pause, the silence stretching between them. Subrato stood there, staring at her, as if trying to understand what she was saying. Asmita turned away, not able to bear the look in his eyes anymore. She walked toward the door, the weight of the night settling in her chest like a heavy stone.

"I'll give you some space, Asmita," Subrato finally said, his voice quieter now. "But I don't know if I can change."

Asmita didn't respond. She grabbed her coat and stepped out of the apartment, feeling the cold air hit her skin like a slap in the face. As she walked away, her heart felt heavy, but there was also a sense of clarity. This wasn't who she was anymore. And she couldn't let anyone—least of all someone who loved her in a way that wasn't truly love—take that away from her.

The night was long, and as she walked alone through the streets, the echoes of her relationship with Subrato reverberated in her mind. But for the first time in a long while, Asmita felt like she was finally taking back control.

SIX

THE BREAKING POINT

The early morning light filtered through the curtains of Subrato's apartment, but Asmita wasn't there to witness it. She had left before the sun had fully risen, gathering only the essentials from their shared space—the things that mattered most to her. Her heart was heavy, but there was a newfound sense of clarity in her chest. She had made the decision, and there was no going back. She couldn't stay with him any longer.

She took a deep breath as she closed the door behind her, stepping into the cool morning air. The weight of the night's altercation still hung over her, but it had pushed her toward something she knew she had been avoiding for far too long.

With each step, she felt a mix of relief and fear, but there was something liberating about leaving the apartment, leaving Subrato behind. She didn't look back.

By the time she reached Sangeeta's apartment, the streets were beginning to bustle with the quiet hum of the city coming to life. Asmita's hands shook as she knocked on the door, her heart racing with anticipation. She had nowhere else to go, no one else to turn to.

Sangeeta opened the door a few moments later, her eyes widening in surprise at the sight of Asmita standing there in the hallway, her face pale, her eyes red-rimmed. It was clear that something had happened, something big.

"Asmi? What's going on? Why are you here so early?" Sangeeta asked, her voice filled with concern. She quickly stepped aside to let her in. "Come in, come in, you're shaking."

Without a word, Asmita walked inside and collapsed onto the couch, her breath coming in quick, shallow gasps. She looked up at Sangeeta with tears in her eyes. "I can't stay with him anymore, Sangeeta. I've left him for good."

Sangeeta froze for a moment, processing what she had just heard. Asmita's voice was raw, her emotions laid bare. "What? What do you mean?" Sangeeta asked, rushing to sit beside her. "Calm down, okay? Take a breath."

"I can't stay with him anymore," Asmita repeated, her voice breaking. "I left. I packed my things, and I left. I just couldn't do it anymore."

Sangeeta's heart ached for her friend. She could see the pain and exhaustion in Asmita's eyes, but she also sensed something else—strength, a decision that had been made in the quiet of her heart. "Okay," Sangeeta said softly, trying to steady her own nerves. "Let's take this one step at a time. You need to settle down first."

Sangeeta stood up and moved to the kitchen. She quickly made a pot of tea, pouring a steaming cup for Asmita and bringing it back to her. "Here," she said, handing the cup to her. "Drink this, and we'll talk."

Asmita took a sip, the warmth of the tea doing little to soothe the storm inside her, but she tried to calm her racing thoughts. Her hands trembled as she set the cup down on the table, her gaze never leaving Sangeeta's concerned face.

"I don't even know where to start," Asmita whispered, wiping a tear from her cheek. "Last night... it all just came to a head. We were at the party, and everything was fine at first. But then he started getting upset. I don't know, Sangeeta—he was angry about me being too close to his friends. He didn't like that they were complimenting my cooking. He was annoyed because I drank more than usual. But the worst part was when he started talking about how I was too happy around them, like I should only be happy with him. Like I should only care about him."

Sangeeta's face hardened with concern. "He said that?"

"Yes," Asmita replied, her voice trembling. "And it wasn't the first time. There have been so many little things before, things that bothered me, but I kept quiet. I told myself I was being unreasonable, that I should just let it go. But last night, it was too much. He made me feel like I didn't belong to him, like my happiness—my friends, my life outside of him—wasn't allowed. And I just couldn't do it anymore. I can't keep compromising my happiness for someone who can't see me for who I am."

Sangeeta sat quietly, absorbing everything Asmita had said. She had always known there were cracks in the relationship, but hearing the details now, the way Asmita spoke of it all—it was clear that this wasn't just a rough patch. This was something deeper, something unhealthy.

"I've been ignoring it for so long," Asmita continued, her voice barely above a whisper. "The possessiveness, the jealousy, the way he controlled everything I did. Even the small things—he didn't like that I drank, didn't like when I laughed too loud with my friends. But last night, it was the breaking point. I don't want to live like that anymore."

Sangeeta's heart ached for her friend. "You didn't deserve that, Asmi. No one does. You have every right to be yourself, to enjoy life without feeling like you're walking on eggshells all the time."

Asmita nodded, the tears still falling down her cheeks. "I just kept thinking maybe it would get better, that maybe I was overreacting. But I'm not, Sangeeta. This is who he is. And it's not right."

Sangeeta took Asmita's hand in hers, squeezing it gently. "You're so strong for making that decision, Asmi. It's not easy. But you did the right thing. You don't owe anyone a life that makes you feel small or suffocated."

Asmita wiped her face with the back of her hand. "I just feel so lost right now. I thought he was the one. I thought we were building something together, but now I'm questioning everything."

"You're not alone, Asmi," Sangeeta said, her voice full of warmth and reassurance. "You have me, and we'll figure this out together. One step at a time. Don't rush yourself to have all the answers. Right now, just focus on healing. And know that you're not the only one who's been through something like this. You'll get through it."

Asmita nodded, her eyes filled with a mixture of exhaustion and relief. "Thank you, Sangeeta. I don't know what I would do without you."

Sangeeta smiled softly. "You'll never have to find out. I'm always here for you. Always."

The two sat in silence for a few moments, the weight of the night still heavy in the air, but somehow lighter now that Asmita had made the decision to leave. The first step had been taken, and though the road ahead would be difficult, Asmita knew she wasn't walking it alone.

And for the first time in a long while, Asmita felt like she had reclaimed a piece of herself. She wasn't sure what the future held, but for now, she was free. Free to rebuild, to heal, and to live life on her own terms. And that was all she needed to know.

Sangeeta sat quietly beside Asmita, her hand still gently resting on her friend's. She watched her intently as she took another slow sip of tea, her eyes still red-rimmed from the sleepless night and the emotional whirlwind she'd been through. The apartment was quiet now, a stark contrast to the storm that had torn through Asmita's heart in the last twenty-four hours.

After a long pause, Sangeeta finally spoke, her voice soft but probing. "Asmi," she said, her eyes steady on Asmita's face, "do you still love him?"

Asmita's eyes flickered, and she seemed to hesitate for a moment. She lowered her gaze, tracing the rim of her tea cup with her finger before she answered. "Yes," she said, her voice barely above a whisper. "I loved him. Maybe too much."

Sangeeta waited, sensing that Asmita wasn't finished. She could tell there was more to it, something deeper that Asmita hadn't fully unpacked yet.

Asmita took a deep breath, her voice faltering slightly. "I loved him so much that I let so many things slide. I tolerated the little signs that something was off, the controlling behavior. I thought maybe it would get better. I kept making excuses for him because I believed he loved me, and I thought that was enough. But now, I realize that love—his love, at least—has turned into something else. Something suffocating."

Sangeeta's gaze softened. "But you don't love him anymore?"

"I don't know if I can say that," Asmita replied, her voice cracking. "I still care about him in some way. I don't think you just stop loving someone overnight. But I can't stay with him, not like this. His love is so intense, so all-consuming, that it's not love anymore, it's possessiveness. And it's destroying everything I am."

Sangeeta nodded slowly, her heart aching for her friend. "So, what now, Asmi? What happens after you leave him behind?"

Asmita looked down at her hands, her fingers trembling slightly as she clasped them together tightly. "I don't know, Sangeeta. I feel lost. I feel like I gave up so much of myself for him, and now... now I'm not even sure who I am without him. But I know one thing for sure—this isn't healthy. I can't keep living with a person who sees me as something to own. I'm not a possession."

Sangeeta reached out, placing her hand gently on Asmita's. "But you're free now, Asmi. You made the hardest decision. It's going to be painful, but in the end, it's for your own well-being."

Asmita nodded, wiping away a tear that had slipped down her cheek. "I thought I could handle it. I thought I could make it work. But I can't anymore, Sangeeta. I tried so hard to love him in a way that made him feel safe, but all it did was push me into a corner where I wasn't allowed to be myself. He loved me so much that he couldn't see that his love was slowly killing me."

Sangeeta stayed silent for a moment, letting Asmita's words sink in. Then, she asked quietly, "So, what do you need now, Asmi? What do you want?"

Asmita took a deep breath, her mind still whirling from the gravity of what she'd just revealed. "I need space. I need to find myself again. I need to remember who I am without him, to rebuild the pieces of me that I lost while trying to make this relationship work. And I need time. Time to heal, to understand what I really want and need in life, without the weight of his love pulling me in every direction."

Sangeeta nodded, her heart full of empathy for her friend. "And you'll have that time, Asmi. You don't have to rush this process. We'll take it one step at a time. And I'll be here, every step of the way."

Asmita smiled faintly, but there was a sadness in her eyes that wouldn't fade. "Thank you, Sangeeta. I don't know what I would do without you."

Sangeeta squeezed her hand again, giving her a soft, reassuring smile. "You'll never have to find out. I'm here for you, always. And we'll get through this together."

For a moment, the two sat there in silence, the weight of the conversation still lingering in the air. Asmita felt the small spark of relief that came with finally making the decision to leave Subrato, but she also knew the road ahead wouldn't be easy. There would be moments of doubt, moments of weakness, but she had made the right choice. She had to remind herself of that.

Finally, Sangeeta spoke again, breaking the silence. "Asmi, I know this is hard to hear right now, but I want you to think about something. Do you think that if Subrato didn't love you so intensely, so possessively, that you would have been able to tolerate this for so long?"

Asmita paused, considering Sangeeta's words. It was a question she hadn't fully allowed herself to think about until now. "Maybe not," she admitted slowly. "Maybe if he didn't love me so much, I wouldn't have stayed. I would have walked away sooner. But his love... it was like a drug, Sangeeta. It felt so good to be adored like that, to feel wanted so deeply. I thought it meant something, that it proved how much he cared about me."

Sangeeta nodded knowingly. "But that kind of love—it's not love, is it? It's possession. And you can't live in a relationship where you're just a thing to be owned. You need a love that sets you free, not one that keeps you locked in a cage."

Asmita's eyes glistened with tears as she looked at her friend. "You're right, Sangeeta. I don't want to feel like that anymore. I don't want to feel suffocated."

Sangeeta smiled softly, squeezing her hand once more. "You're going to be okay, Asmi. It's going to take time, but we'll get through this. I'll be here with you, every step of the way. And you'll find your strength again. You've already made the hardest decision."

Asmita nodded, her heart still heavy, but there was a flicker of hope beginning to take root. For the first time in a long while, she felt a sense of ownership over her own life again. And though the road ahead would be uncertain, she knew she wasn't alone. Not anymore.

SEVEN
THE UNSPOKEN TRUTHS

It had been two days since Asmita left Subrato's apartment, and though she hadn't looked back, her heart still felt heavy. Staying at Sangeeta's apartment provided a small sense of comfort, but the weight of everything still loomed over her. She couldn't bring herself to go back to her parents' house—not yet, not with everything still so raw. She didn't want to involve them in her breakup, not until she was ready to face it herself.

Sangeeta had insisted, of course, that Asmita stay with her for as long as she needed. "You're not going anywhere, Asmi. You're staying here, with me, until you get your feet back on the ground," Sangeeta had said the first night Asmita arrived. "I know things are hard right now, but you don't have to face them alone."

Asmita had been reluctant at first. It wasn't that she didn't appreciate Sangeeta's kindness, but she felt guilty for being a burden. But Sangeeta insisted, as always, and Asmita was too tired to argue. They both knew that Sangeeta's apartment—small, cozy, and filled with the scent of vanilla candles—was a sanctuary. Sangeeta lived alone, and for now, Asmita was content to share her space.

That evening, Sangeeta suggested, "Why don't you sleep in the spare bedroom tonight? You deserve your space." But Asmita had shaken her head, her lips curving into a faint smile. "No, I'm fine. Let's just share your bed tonight. It'll be nice to just talk."

Sangeeta's face brightened, a warm smile spreading across her face. "Of course. We can have a proper girls' night in. Wine, gossip, and, of course, talking things out."

As the night settled in, the two women lay side by side on Sangeeta's bed, glasses of wine in hand, the soft hum of the city outside their window. The room was filled with a comfortable silence, broken only by the occasional clink of their glasses.

Asmita glanced over at Sangeeta, her mind swirling with the thoughts and emotions that had been clouding her for days. "Sangeeta," she began hesitantly, "the session with Paromita went well. She's really kind, and I think I'm going to keep seeing her."

Sangeeta turned toward her, her expression attentive. "That's great, Asmi. I'm glad it helped. You really need someone to talk to about all of this."

Asmita nodded, but there was something in her voice that didn't quite match her words. "It did. I mean, it helped to talk about what I've been feeling. But... I didn't really get into everything. I didn't talk about Subrato much, or the details of our relationship."

Sangeeta raised an eyebrow. "You didn't? Why not?"

Asmita sighed, the weight of her past relationship pressing down on her chest. "I don't know. It's just... hard to talk about. There's so much I've been holding in for so long, and I'm not sure where to start. I mean, where do I even begin? The whole thing feels like a blur now."

Sangeeta set her glass of wine down on the nightstand and turned to face Asmita fully, her eyes filled with understanding. "I get it, Asmi. I really do. But you have to talk about it. Step by step. You can't keep bottling it up inside. Especially not now."

"I know," Asmita replied softly, her voice quiet and almost apologetic. "It's just... there's so much. I don't even know if I want to relive all of it."

Sangeeta reached out and took Asmita's hand gently, giving it a reassuring squeeze. "You don't have to do it all at once. You can take it slow. But you need to open up, bit by bit, or else it'll keep eating at you."

Asmita closed her eyes, leaning back against the pillows as a soft sigh escaped her lips. "I just feel so... lost. Like I'm stuck in the middle of everything, and I don't know how to move forward. I left Subrato, but a part of me still feels attached to him. And I hate that feeling."

Sangeeta's voice was soft but firm. "It's okay to feel that way, Asmi. It's normal. But you have to let go of him, of everything that came with him. If you keep holding on to that, you won't be able to move forward."

Asmita turned her head to look at Sangeeta, her expression vulnerable. "I know. I just... I keep questioning myself. Did I make the right choice? Was I too harsh? I mean, Subrato loved me so much. He was obsessed with me, in a way that made him clingy and possessive. I know he wanted to keep me for himself, but part of me still feels like I'm abandoning him."

Sangeeta leaned in closer, her voice gentle but firm. "You didn't abandon him, Asmi. You're taking care of yourself. There's nothing wrong with that. His love was controlling, not love. And you didn't deserve to feel suffocated like that.

You needed to set yourself free."

Asmita nodded, though the doubts still lingered in the back of her mind. "I know you're right, but it doesn't feel that simple. Every time I think about what happened, about what I've lost... it feels like I've made the biggest mistake of my life. But at the same time, I know I couldn't keep living like that."

Sangeeta rested her hand on Asmita's arm, offering her comfort without words. "You didn't make a mistake, Asmi. You made a choice. A hard choice, but one that's necessary for your happiness. You can't keep sacrificing yourself for someone else's version of love."

There was a long pause as Asmita absorbed Sangeeta's words. She felt a small knot in her chest begin to loosen, just a little. The warmth of the wine, the softness of the bed, and the presence of her best friend next to her created a small sense of peace she hadn't felt in days.

Finally, Asmita spoke again, her voice quieter this time. "I guess I need to open up more, don't I? To Paromita, to you, to myself. But it's hard. Every time I think about telling someone everything... it feels like it's too much to carry."

Sangeeta nodded, her expression empathetic. "It's a process, Asmi. You don't have to share everything at once. Take it one step at a time, and soon enough, you'll find the strength to face it all. But you're not alone. Not anymore."

Asmita squeezed Sangeeta's hand, feeling a small weight lift from her shoulders. "Thank you, Sangeeta. I don't know what I'd do without you."

Sangeeta smiled warmly, brushing a stray lock of hair from Asmita's forehead. "You don't have to find out, Asmi. I'm right here. Always."

As they lay there, the soft glow of the evening casting a warm light over the room, Asmita realized that the road ahead would be difficult, but she no longer had to face it alone. The first steps had been taken, and she was starting to feel the faintest glimmer of hope. It was a long road to recovery, but she was no longer walking it in darkness.

As the night wore on and the soft glow of the lamp cast shadows over the room, the two friends continued to talk, each finding solace in sharing their thoughts, fears, and unspoken truths. Asmita felt a little lighter with each passing minute, but she knew there was still so much she had to work through. Sangeeta, sensing that Asmita needed a distraction, smiled softly and shifted the conversation.

"You know, Asmi," Sangeeta began, her tone a bit more playful now, "I'm not all that great with relationships either."

Asmita raised an eyebrow. "What do you mean?"

Sangeeta took a deep breath, staring up at the ceiling as if gathering her thoughts. "Well, after a couple of breakups, I just kind of... gave up on guys. I got so frustrated with them, with how things never seemed to work out the way I wanted. And, honestly, I got tired of feeling hurt. So, I decided to stop taking them seriously, just stopped expecting anything good to come out of it."

Asmita listened intently, her curiosity piqued. "So, what did you do instead?"

Sangeeta chuckled, a bitter edge to her laugh. "I decided to stay single. Just live my life on my own terms, you know? But whenever I feel lonely, or when I get down, I sometimes end up on one of those random dating apps." She looked at Asmita and shrugged. "It's like a temporary distraction, but I don't really take it seriously. I don't think I could, even if I tried."

Asmita was quiet for a moment, reflecting on Sangeeta's words. She could hear the pain behind the laughter, the years of disappointment that had led Sangeeta to build a wall around her heart. But then Sangeeta added something that made Asmita's heart ache with empathy.

"Recently, though, I've been realizing something," Sangeeta continued, her voice softer now. "I've become way closer to my girl friends. I don't know, Asmi... there's something about being around women. They never say anything to hurt me, never make me feel small. We talk about everything, and I find myself opening up more to my girls than I ever did to any guy."

Asmita looked at her in surprise. "You've always been such a romantic, though. I thought you'd still be looking for 'the one.'"

Sangeeta laughed again, a little louder this time. "I was, once. But I'm starting to think that maybe I'm just not wired for it. Or maybe... maybe I just haven't found someone who gets me the way my friends do." She paused for a moment, her voice turning more introspective. "To be honest, I'm not even sure about my sexual orientation right now. I mean, I never really thought about it before, but lately, it's been something I've wondered about."

Asmita blinked in surprise, her expression softening with understanding. "You mean... you don't know if you like men or women, or both?"

Sangeeta nodded, her lips twitching into a smile. "Yeah, exactly. I guess I've just been so focused on relationships, on the idea of what I'm 'supposed' to want, that I never took the time to figure out what I actually want. Who I am."

Asmita's eyes softened with empathy. "That's a huge thing to realize. But it's good that you're thinking about it. Don't rush yourself, Sangeeta. Just take your time."

Sangeeta smiled, her expression becoming a little lighter, a little more playful. "I mean, it's all pretty funny, right? Here I am, questioning everything about myself, and the only thing I know for sure is that I'm completely in love with my best friend." She paused, then laughed at herself. "You're probably rolling your eyes at me right now."

Asmita looked at Sangeeta, her face softening with affection. "I'm not rolling my eyes," she said, her voice warm. "I'm just glad you're finally being honest with yourself. That's the most important thing. And no matter what you figure out, I'm here for you. You know that, right?"

Sangeeta looked at her with a mixture of tenderness and vulnerability. "Thanks, Asmi. You have no idea how much that means to me. I've always felt like I had to figure everything out on my own, but tonight... it feels like a huge weight has been lifted just by talking to you."

Asmita smiled softly, her heart swelling with warmth. "You're not alone, Sangeeta. You never have been."

There was a brief, comfortable silence between them, and for a moment, the only sound in the room was the quiet hum of the city outside. Then, as if on impulse, Sangeeta turned to face Asmita, her eyes shining with affection.

"You know, you're the best," Sangeeta said, her voice light but filled with sincerity.

Asmita looked at her, her lips curving into a smile. "I think you're the best, too."

Sangeeta smiled brightly and, without warning, leaned over to hug Asmita tightly. "I love you, Asmi," she said, her voice muffled in the embrace.

Asmita hugged her back, her own arms wrapping around Sangeeta with a sense of deep affection and gratitude. "I love you too, Sangeeta."

And then, as if unable to resist, Sangeeta pulled back slightly and kissed Asmita on the cheek, her lips soft against her skin. "You know," she said with a mischievous grin, "I think I'm actually a little bit in love with you too."

Asmita laughed, the sound light and full of warmth, before playfully pushing Sangeeta away. "You're impossible," she said, but there was no mistaking the affection in her voice.

Sangeeta rolled her eyes dramatically. "I'm just being honest, okay?"

Asmita smiled, feeling the first genuine spark of joy in days. "Well, I'll take that honesty any day."

As the two of them settled back into the bed, the conversation turning back to lighter topics, Asmita couldn't help but feel a deep sense of relief. She was surrounded by people who cared for her, and she was starting to realize that, for the first time in a long while, she was allowed to be herself—whole, unburdened, and loved.

And maybe, just maybe, that was all she needed for now.

EIGHT

THE HEALING ROOM

Asmita sat comfortably in the soft chair across from Paromita's desk, her legs crossed as she tucked her hands into her lap. The faint smell of lavender and calming incense filled the air, the soft hum of a distant air conditioner adding to the serene atmosphere of Paromita's private therapy room. The walls, painted in warm beige tones, were adorned with simple artwork, offering a peaceful ambiance that helped ease Asmita's nerves. The space felt safe, inviting, like a sanctuary where she could explore her deepest thoughts and emotions without judgment.

Paromita, dressed in her usual calming, professional attire, was sitting across from her, her eyes sharp but kind as she watched Asmita settle into the chair. She smiled gently, encouraging Asmita to relax.

"So, Asmita," Paromita began, her voice soothing but firm, "I'm glad you've decided to come back today. You've made a lot of progress already, and I think we can start getting deeper into what's really going on with you."

Asmita nodded, feeling a bit more at ease. She had always trusted Paromita, especially given how open and non-judgmental the psychologist was. She felt like she was finally ready to explore what was happening inside her head.

"I'm ready, Paromita," Asmita said softly, her voice betraying a hint of nervousness.

Paromita leaned forward slightly, her tone becoming more informative as she began to talk. "Today, I want to give you a broader understanding of what depression really is. It's not just about feeling down or sad. Depression is a complex, multi-faceted condition that affects both the mind and the body. It's the root cause of many forms of psychosis, including schizophrenia, and it's often misdiagnosed or misunderstood. But understanding its full impact is crucial to recognizing how it affects different aspects of a person's life."

Asmita listened intently, her gaze focused on Paromita as she spoke.

"Clinical depression," Paromita continued, "is more than just feeling sad or low. It's a medical condition, one that often has deep biological, psychological, and social roots. It can manifest in a variety of ways, such as persistent feelings of sadness, hopelessness, and worthlessness, but it can also involve physical symptoms, such as fatigue, sleep disturbances, changes in appetite, and loss of interest in activities you once enjoyed. And the thing about clinical depression is that it's not something you can will away. It's not about pulling yourself together. It's a condition that requires treatment—whether that be through therapy, medication, or a combination of both."

Asmita nodded slowly, absorbing the information. She had always known depression was more than just sadness, but hearing it articulated so clearly made it feel even more real, more tangible.

"Why do you think depression often leads to psychosis, or even schizophrenia?" Asmita asked, genuinely curious.

Paromita smiled softly, appreciating Asmita's interest in understanding the complexities of the condition. "Well, depression, particularly when left untreated, can cause significant changes in the brain's chemistry and functioning. It affects neurotransmitters—chemicals that help nerve cells communicate with each other. The most well-known of these are serotonin, dopamine, and norepinephrine. When these chemicals are out of balance, it can lead to a range of psychological issues. Over time, chronic depression can also trigger psychosis, a disconnection from reality. People with severe, untreated depression might experience hallucinations, delusions, or even a complete breakdown of their ability to distinguish what is real and what isn't."

Asmita listened in quiet awe. The idea that depression could be the precursor to such severe psychological conditions was a concept she had never fully considered.

Paromita paused for a moment, letting the information sink in, before continuing, "Schizophrenia, for instance, is often misdiagnosed in the early stages because it can present with symptoms similar to depression—like a lack of energy or motivation, and a sense of emotional numbness. But schizophrenia involves a more complex disconnection from reality, and it can have a devastating impact on one's ability to function in the world. The lines between depression and other disorders can be blurry, which is why it's so important to get a proper diagnosis and treatment early on."

Asmita absorbed the gravity of Paromita's words, feeling a mix of understanding and concern. "So, if someone doesn't get help for depression, it could turn into something even more serious?"

Paromita nodded gravely. "Yes, it can. But that's why we're here. To catch these signs early and address them before they escalate. You're taking the right steps by being here, by acknowledging what you're going through. It's not an easy path, but it's the one that will help you regain control over your life."

Asmita took a deep breath, feeling a sense of relief that she was in good hands. "It helps to understand it like this," she said quietly. "It makes it feel less... scary."

Paromita smiled, her tone softening. "I'm glad to hear that. The more you understand about depression and its effects, the more empowered you'll feel in managing it. And you'll also be better equipped to recognize when it's becoming something more than just sadness, something that requires intervention."

With a thoughtful pause, Paromita continued, "I want to take a moment to talk about the history of depression, as well. Depression isn't a new phenomenon. In fact, it's been recognized for centuries, although it wasn't always understood the way we do today. The ancient Greeks referred to it as 'melancholia,' and the term has evolved over time. It was once believed to be a result of an imbalance of bodily fluids, specifically black bile. But over the years, research in the fields of psychology and psychiatry has given us a much clearer understanding of depression."

She leaned back in her chair, her fingers drumming gently on the table. "Renowned psychiatrists like Sigmund Freud, Aaron Beck, and Carl Rogers have contributed immensely to our understanding of depression. Freud believed that depression could be a result of unresolved internal conflicts, while Beck's cognitive theory focused on the negative thought patterns that perpetuate depression. Rogers, on the other hand, was all about the therapeutic relationship, emphasizing the importance of empathy and unconditional positive regard in helping someone through their depression."

Asmita's eyes widened as she took in the wealth of knowledge that Paromita was sharing. "So, all these psychiatrists contributed to how we understand depression today?"

"Exactly," Paromita said with a nod. "Their work was groundbreaking, and their contributions continue to influence how we approach therapy and mental health care today. Depression isn't just a personal struggle—it's something that affects society at large, which is why it's important to keep learning about it, to keep studying it, so we can better help people who are suffering."

Asmita sat quietly, feeling the weight of the knowledge Paromita had just shared with her. For the first time in a while, she felt like she had a better grasp on what was happening inside her mind. She understood that depression wasn't something she could simply push away, and that it wasn't a sign of weakness. It was an illness, one that required care, attention, and treatment—just like any physical illness.

"I'm glad I came to see you, Paromita," Asmita said, her voice sincere. "I feel like I'm starting to understand myself better. And maybe... just maybe, I'm not so alone in all of this."

Paromita smiled warmly, her eyes soft with compassion. "You're never alone, Asmita. And you're doing the right thing by seeking help. We'll take this one step at a time, together. I'm here for you, every step of the way."

As Asmita looked at Paromita, she felt a flicker of hope for the first time in weeks. There was still a long road ahead, but now, she knew she wasn't walking it alone. She had support. She had knowledge. And, most importantly, she had the strength to keep moving forward.

As the session continued, Paromita's tone shifted, becoming more clinical, but with the same warmth and care that made Asmita feel at ease. She could tell that Paromita wanted to empower her with more knowledge, to help her understand not only what was going on in her mind, but also how science and medicine could play a role in healing.

"Asmita," Paromita began, her voice steady, "now that we've talked about the psychological aspects of depression, let's delve a bit deeper into the medical side of things—specifically the treatments. Medicine is an essential component of treatment for many people suffering from depression, and it's important to understand how it works, and why therapy alone sometimes isn't enough."

Asmita leaned forward slightly, her interest piqued. She had been curious about medications for depression but hadn't quite understood how they worked. "Okay, I'm listening," she said, her voice eager for answers.

Paromita smiled and nodded. "There are a number of medications used to treat depression, and they work in different ways, depending on the type of depression and the individual's response to the drug. The main goal of antidepressant medications is to correct imbalances in neurotransmitters—the chemicals in your brain that regulate mood, sleep, appetite, and other important functions."

She paused for a moment to make sure Asmita was following along. "The most commonly prescribed types of antidepressants are Selective Serotonin Reuptake Inhibitors, or SSRIs, and Serotonin-Norepinephrine Reuptake Inhibitors, or SNRIs. These medications work by increasing the levels of serotonin and norepinephrine in the brain, which are neurotransmitters that help regulate mood and stress."

"That sounds complicated," Asmita said, her brow furrowing in curiosity. "How exactly do they do that?"

Paromita nodded understandingly. "It's a bit complex, but I'll break it down for you. Essentially, serotonin and norepinephrine are chemicals in your brain that transmit signals between nerve cells. In a person with depression, the levels of these neurotransmitters are often lower than they should be. SSRIs and SNRIs work by blocking the reabsorption—or reuptake—of these chemicals, allowing them to stay in the brain longer, which improves mood and reduces symptoms of depression."

"Are there other kinds of medications?" Asmita asked, her curiosity growing.

Paromita leaned back in her chair, folding her arms gently. "Yes, there are several other classes of medications used in treating depression. For example, there are Tricyclic Antidepressants (TCAs), which are among the oldest antidepressants, and Monoamine Oxidase Inhibitors (MAOIs). TCAs work similarly to SSRIs but tend to have more side effects, which is why they're not as commonly prescribed anymore. MAOIs work by blocking the enzyme monoamine oxidase, which breaks down serotonin, norepinephrine, and dopamine. However, these can also have significant dietary restrictions and side effects, so they're typically only used when other medications haven't worked."

As she spoke, Paromita's hands moved in fluid motions, as if drawing the picture of how the medications worked in the brain. "There's also a newer class of medications called Atypical Antidepressants, which don't fit into the other categories but can be effective for some people. These medications, like bupropion, work in different ways to affect neurotransmitters and can sometimes be used in combination with other antidepressants for a more comprehensive approach."

Asmita nodded, trying to absorb all the information. "I see. So, what kind of medications are typically prescribed these days?"

Paromita smiled and nodded. "Currently, SSRIs and SNRIs are the most commonly prescribed antidepressants, and for good reason. They tend to have fewer side effects compared to older medications, and they're effective for a wide range of people. Some examples of SSRIs include fluoxetine (Prozac), sertraline (Zoloft), and escitalopram (Lexapro). SNRIs include venlafaxine (Effexor) and duloxetine (Cymbalta). These are typically the first-line treatments for depression."

"But what about side effects?" Asmita asked, still uncertain about the potential downsides of taking these medications.

Paromita leaned forward, her expression serious yet empathetic. "It's an important question, and you're right to be cautious. Like any medication, antidepressants do have side effects. Some of the most common ones include nausea, headaches, dry mouth, and changes in sleep patterns. Some people also experience sexual side effects, like reduced libido or difficulty achieving orgasm, which can be distressing."

She paused, her gaze softening. "However, it's important to remember that not everyone will experience these side effects, and if they do occur, they often lessen after a few weeks. Additionally, some people may find that the benefits far outweigh the side effects. But this is why it's essential to have ongoing discussions with your doctor, especially when starting a new medication."

Asmita absorbed this information, her mind working through the possibilities. "What if I don't want to take medication? Can therapy alone really help?"

Paromita's expression softened, and she nodded understandingly. "Therapy is an essential component of treatment for depression. In fact, Cognitive Behavioral Therapy (CBT) has been shown to be highly effective in treating depression, especially in combination with medication. Therapy helps you recognize and change negative thought patterns that contribute to depression, and it also gives you tools to manage stress and difficult emotions."

"Can therapy alone cure depression?" Asmita asked, unsure of what to believe.

Paromita hesitated, choosing her words carefully. "For some people, therapy alone can be incredibly helpful, and in mild to moderate cases of depression, it can be enough to help you manage and recover. However, for more severe cases, or when depression has been ongoing for a long time, therapy alone may not be enough. This is where medications come in. They help restore the balance in the brain, while therapy helps you address the emotional and psychological components of the illness."

As she spoke, Paromita's voice was firm but compassionate. "The key to successful treatment is often a combination of both. The medication helps stabilize you enough to engage fully in therapy, and therapy can help you understand and cope with the changes happening in your brain. It's a holistic approach."

Asmita nodded slowly, processing this new understanding. "I think I'm starting to get it. The medication isn't a quick fix, but it helps address the biological side of things so therapy can work more effectively."

"Exactly," Paromita affirmed. "You're not just treating the symptoms—you're working to restore balance, and that takes time. It's not a quick process, but it is a process, and it's one you're fully capable of navigating with the right tools."

Asmita sat back in her chair, feeling a sense of relief that she hadn't expected. The complex world of depression and its treatment was starting to make sense. "Thank you, Paromita," she said quietly. "This really helps. I feel more prepared to deal with it now."

Paromita smiled warmly. "I'm glad, Asmita. You've made a lot of progress just by understanding what's going on inside of you. And remember, you don't have to figure it all out today. You're taking the right steps, and I'm here to guide you through it."

Asmita smiled, a sense of calm settling over her. "I'll keep that in mind. One step at a time, right?"

"Exactly," Paromita replied, her tone warm and reassuring. "One step at a time."

As Asmita left the session, she felt a weight lifting from her shoulders. The path ahead was still uncertain, but for the first time in a long while, she felt confident that she was on the right track, with the knowledge and support she needed to face the challenges ahead.

NINE

BEHIND THE MASK OF DEPRESSION

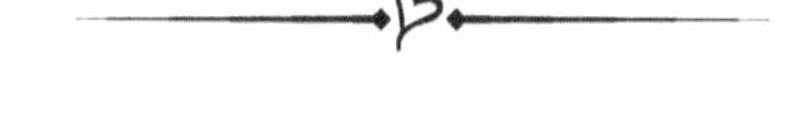

The evening had settled into a comfortable rhythm, with soft jazz playing in the background and the warmth of candlelight flickering across the room. Asmita and Sangeeta had spent the last few hours preparing a simple but hearty dinner, one that felt more like a gathering of old friends than a formal meal. The smell of roasted vegetables and freshly cooked pasta filled the air, and the table was set with care, the glasses ready for the wine they had picked out earlier.

"This feels so much better than sitting in an office," Asmita said, a smile tugging at her lips as she looked across at Sangeeta. "I mean, it's nice to get out of that formal space and just talk, you know?"

Sangeeta grinned, her eyes bright. "Definitely. I think we both need a little break from the usual routine, and I'm excited to have Paromita join us. It'll be good to finally ask her those questions we've been wondering about, outside the confines of a therapy session."

Asmita nodded, a mixture of curiosity and anticipation bubbling inside her. "Yeah, I've been thinking about the things we discussed last time, about the chemicals in the brain and how depression works. I really want to understand more, especially about the triggers. I mean, it's all so much to process, right?"

Sangeeta leaned back, her eyes thoughtful. "Exactly. I think talking with Paromita in this informal way will give us a better understanding of the big picture—what triggers those chemical imbalances, and why some people are more vulnerable than others."

Just then, the doorbell rang, and Sangeeta hopped up to greet Paromita, who had arrived with a warm smile and a bottle of wine in hand.

"Good evening!" Paromita said cheerfully, holding the wine out to Asmita as she entered the apartment. "I come bearing wine. It's nice to finally sit down and have this conversation outside the therapy room."

"Perfect timing!" Sangeeta said, gesturing to the table. "We were just getting things ready. Dinner's almost ready. Let's pop open that bottle and relax."

They all gathered around the table, the mood light and casual. As they settled in, Paromita poured the wine, and the three of them clinked glasses.

"Here's to good company and even better conversation," Paromita said with a smile.

The evening began with light conversation, catching up on personal lives, but soon, the real discussion began. After a few sips of wine, Asmita, eager to dive into the topic that had been weighing on her mind, leaned forward.

"Paromita, I've been thinking a lot about what we discussed in our last session," she began, her voice a little more serious now. "About how depression can be caused by chemical imbalances in the brain. But there's something I'm still not clear on. If people have the same fault lines in their brain—like, say, the same chemical imbalances—does that automatically mean they're going to develop depression or other mental health issues? Or are there other factors involved?"

Paromita looked thoughtfully at her glass for a moment before responding, her voice calm and measured. "That's an excellent question, Asmita. And it's one that touches on some of the most important aspects of mental health. Let me explain it a bit more."

She set her glass down and leaned forward slightly, preparing to speak in more detail.

"First of all," Paromita began, "it's important to understand that everyone has a unique neurobiological makeup. The brain is incredibly complex, and the chemicals that regulate mood—serotonin, dopamine, norepinephrine—are influenced by a variety of factors, both genetic and environmental. These neurotransmitters play a key role in controlling emotions, thought processes, and behavior."

She paused, allowing the information to sink in, then continued. "Some people are born with a predisposition to certain chemical imbalances. These imbalances, as we discussed earlier, can contribute to depression or other mental health issues. But that doesn't mean that someone with a genetic predisposition will definitely develop a mental illness. It's all about the interplay between genetic factors and environmental triggers."

Sangeeta, always the curious one, jumped in. "So, you're saying that just because someone has these 'fault lines' in their brain, it doesn't guarantee they'll suffer from depression?"

Paromita nodded. "Exactly. It's all about the environmental factors—stress, trauma, life events, and even ongoing lifestyle choices—that can trigger or exacerbate the imbalances in the brain. For example, a person might have a genetic predisposition to depression, but if they don't experience any major stressors or traumatic events, they might not develop the illness. But if that person faces prolonged stress, loss, or isolation, it could trigger the depression."

Asmita's eyes widened as the pieces started to fall into place. "So, is it possible for someone who has the same genetic 'fault lines' but doesn't face these stressors to never develop depression?"

"Yes," Paromita said, her voice steady but with a hint of emphasis. "That's exactly right. A person with a genetic vulnerability might never experience depression if they're able to maintain a healthy environment, supportive relationships, and effective coping strategies. On the other hand, someone without any genetic vulnerabilities but who experiences significant stress might still develop depression."

Sangeeta leaned back, her expression thoughtful. "That makes sense. So, it's not just the brain chemistry—it's the whole context of a person's life that plays a role in whether they develop depression or not."

"Exactly," Paromita replied. "And that's why we need to approach depression in a holistic way. We can't just look at brain chemistry in isolation. We have to consider the person as a whole—their genetics, their environment, their relationships, their life experiences, and even their coping mechanisms."

Asmita took a sip of wine, letting Paromita's words sink in. "But what about therapy? Can therapy alone really help if someone has a brain chemistry imbalance? Or do they always need medication?"

Paromita sighed and set her glass down, her expression turning serious once again. "That's a common misconception. Therapy is incredibly valuable, and in some cases, it can be all that's needed. Cognitive Behavioral Therapy (CBT) is especially effective for people dealing with depression because it helps to reframe negative thinking patterns and provides strategies for managing stress and emotions. But for people with significant chemical imbalances, therapy alone might not be enough."

She paused, looking between Asmita and Sangeeta, her gaze steady. "In cases of moderate to severe depression, medication can play a vital role. Medications like SSRIs or SNRIs work to correct chemical imbalances in the brain, making it easier for the person to engage in therapy and benefit from it. Without the medications, it can be very difficult for someone to fully engage in therapy, especially if they're experiencing constant, overwhelming sadness or a lack of energy."

"That makes sense," Asmita murmured. "So therapy alone won't always cure depression if the chemical imbalance is severe enough."

"Correct," Paromita said, her voice patient and kind. "Medication and therapy work best when combined. The medication addresses the biological side, while therapy helps with the psychological and emotional aspects. It's a balanced approach that has the highest chance of success."

Sangeeta, who had been listening intently, raised another question. "So, does that mean that someone with no irregularity in their brain would never develop depression or any other mental health issue, no matter what happens to them?"

Paromita's expression softened, as she took another moment to choose her words carefully. "That's a tricky question, and unfortunately, no, it's not quite that simple. Even people with no genetic vulnerabilities can still face mental health challenges, especially if they're exposed to extreme stress, trauma, or chronic hardship. Life events can still overwhelm the system. However, people with a well-functioning brain chemistry and solid coping mechanisms are certainly more resilient and less likely to develop severe mental health conditions."

Asmita thought for a moment, absorbing the weight of Paromita's words. "So, there's no 'perfect' protection against mental health issues. No matter how healthy someone's brain chemistry is, they could still face struggles depending on what life throws at them."

"Exactly," Paromita said, her voice reassuring. "Life can be unpredictable, but understanding how to protect your mental health, learning healthy coping mechanisms, and seeking help when needed are essential steps in maintaining emotional balance."

Sangeeta took a deep breath, nodding thoughtfully. "Thank you, Paromita. This really helps us understand the complexities behind mental health. It's not just about one factor, but a combination of everything—biology, environment, experiences, and support."

Asmita smiled, feeling a weight lift off her shoulders. "This has been so enlightening. I feel like I have a much clearer picture now."

Paromita smiled warmly at both of them. "I'm glad. Remember, understanding is the first step toward healing. You both are already on the right path."

As they clinked their glasses together in a toast, the evening felt lighter, and the conversation turned to lighter matters. Yet, even as they laughed and joked, both Asmita and Sangeeta knew that they now had the tools to better understand their own mental health—and the courage to face whatever challenges lay ahead, together.

TEN

"WHY DOES IT HAVE TO BE ME?"

The room was quieter now, the hum of the air conditioner providing a soft backdrop to the silence that hung between Asmita and Paromita. Asmita settled into the recliner that Paromita had directed her to, her body tense, her mind racing. The familiar, comforting scent of lavender filled the room, but it did little to soothe the storm brewing within her.

She had come here today hoping to find clarity, hoping to make sense of the tumultuous emotions that had been flooding her since her breakup with Subrato. But as she sat there, in the comfort of Paromita's office, everything felt more overwhelming than ever. The silence between them felt heavy, like an unspoken truth was waiting to be revealed.

Finally, Asmita could hold it in no longer. She turned sharply toward Paromita, her voice thick with emotion. "Why does it have to be me?" Her words came out as a raw question, full of pain and confusion. She tried to keep it together, but the tears came anyway, slipping down her cheeks despite her best efforts to stay composed.

Paromita, sitting across from her, reached for a box of tissues and handed it to Asmita with a gentle, understanding look. "It's okay, Asmita," she said softly. "You're allowed to feel this way. You're allowed to cry. This isn't easy, but you're not alone."

Asmita took the tissue gratefully, wiping her face with a shaky hand. She could feel the tightness in her chest, the pressure of everything she had been holding back, but somehow hearing Paromita's calm voice made her feel safe enough to let go. She took a deep breath and spoke again, her voice barely above a whisper. "I don't understand. Why is this happening to me? Why did it all fall apart?"

Paromita's expression softened, and she leaned back in her chair, her eyes kind but resolute. "You're not the only one who's ever asked that question, Asmita. Life is full of ups and downs. I can't tell you why it's you—why it's happening now. But I can tell you that you're strong enough to get through it, and I'll be here with you every step of the way."

Asmita looked up at her, wiping away another tear. "I don't know if I can keep going like this, Paromita. It feels like everything is falling apart, like I'm losing control."

"I understand," Paromita said quietly. "But you're not alone. Even I have my own struggles. Life has its way of testing us all."

Asmita's brows furrowed as she looked at her therapist. "What do you mean? What's been so hard for you?"

Paromita paused for a moment, a flash of vulnerability crossing her face before she composed herself. "I've been through my own fair share of heartache, Asmita. My life hasn't been without its struggles. You know, my husband, who is a renowned cardiologist, left me for a young nurse,

He was someone I thought I could trust, someone I thought was perfect. But love doesn't always follow a logical path, does it?"

Asmita was taken aback, her eyes widening with surprise. She had never expected Paromita to share something so personal. "I'm sorry, Paromita," she said softly. "That must have been so painful."

Paromita gave a small nod, her gaze distant for a moment before she looked back at Asmita. "It was. It still hurts, in some ways. I ignored his flings for a long time, thinking that maybe that was his way of coping with stress, but in the end, it was more than I could handle. Things went too far. There were whispers, gossip everywhere, and I knew it wasn't something I could ignore anymore. So, I decided to call it a day."

Asmita listened quietly, unsure of how to respond. She had always viewed Paromita as someone who had her life together, someone strong and grounded. To hear that she had gone through something so deeply painful made Asmita realize just how much more there was to her therapist than she had imagined.

"I took a solo tour through Europe after the breakup," Paromita continued, her voice softening with the memory. "I needed to heal. A month away, alone, helped me clear my head and come to terms with everything. When I came back, I threw myself into my profession, into my work with patients, because that's what kept me grounded. It helped me find purpose again."

Asmita listened closely, her heart aching for Paromita. "And you were able to move on?"

Paromita hesitated for a moment before answering. "I won't say it was easy, or that it was quick. But eventually, I found peace. But I'm not ashamed to admit that, at first,

I struggled. To deal with the trauma, I started taking pills. I knew which ones to take, and for a while, they helped. It was just a way for me to cope with the aftermath, to keep going day by day. It's not something I would recommend, but sometimes, we do what we have to do to survive. I wasn't in therapy at that time, and I felt so lost."

Asmita's eyes widened as she absorbed Paromita's confession. "You took medication? I never would have guessed."

Paromita gave a soft, almost bitter laugh. "People think that therapists and psychiatrists have all the answers, that we have it together all the time. But we're human, too. I've been through pain, and I've had to find my own ways to heal, just like anyone else."

Asmita wiped her eyes again, still processing everything Paromita had just shared. "I never thought about it like that," she admitted. "I always thought therapists were perfect, that they had all the answers."

"We're not perfect," Paromita said, her voice steady but kind. "And sometimes, we need help too. But that doesn't make us less capable of helping others. In fact, it often makes us more understanding and compassionate."

Asmita sat back in the recliner, taking a deep breath. "I guess I've had two breakups in the span of ten years," she said, her voice quieter now. "But those weren't the main reason I feel like this. I'm actually happy I didn't drag those relationships on longer. I think you'd agree with me after you hear my story."

Paromita nodded, her eyes warm and encouraging. "I'm listening, Asmita. And I understand. Breakups are painful, no matter the reason. But it's important to recognize that those experiences—whether they were painful or liberating—don't define you. What matters now is how you move forward from here, how you heal."

Asmita paused for a moment, gathering her thoughts. "I feel like, in some way, I've been avoiding the truth for a long time. I always thought I was strong enough to handle everything, but now... I don't know. I feel broken, Paromita."

"You're not broken," Paromita said gently. "You're just in the process of healing. And that's okay. You're allowed to feel everything you're feeling right now. It's all part of the journey."

Asmita nodded slowly, the weight of Paromita's words sinking in. For the first time, she felt a small spark of hope, a belief that she could heal, that she wasn't alone in this. As she looked at Paromita, she realized that maybe, just maybe, it was possible to come through the pain stronger than before.

"Thank you, Paromita," Asmita said quietly, her voice thick with emotion. "For sharing that with me. And for helping me see that it's okay to not be okay sometimes."

Paromita smiled softly, her eyes kind. "You don't have to do this alone, Asmita. And you're not alone. You're taking the right steps, and I'm here for you, every step of the way."

As the session came to an end, Asmita felt a sense of clarity she hadn't expected. She didn't have all the answers yet, but she was beginning to understand that healing wasn't a straight path—and that it was okay to lean on others along the way.

ELEVEN

THE SHOCK OF BETRAYAL

Asmita sat in the familiar comfort of the recliner, her hands nervously twisting the hem of her sleeve, the conversation with Paromita still fresh in her mind. But as Paromita had so gently explained, sometimes understanding the present required revisiting the past. Asmita knew this was a part of the healing process—accepting what had happened, so she could truly move forward.

The memory crept in, unbidden and sharp.

It was her first serious relationship, and the connection with Tapon had seemed effortless. He was an architect, creative and passionate about his work. They were a perfect match—or so Asmita had believed. Their relationship had always been smooth, full of promises about the future, and everyone knew that marriage was around the corner. Two years had passed, and Asmita couldn't imagine her life without him.

When she went on the week-long office project out of town, everything seemed normal. She had missed him, of course, but it felt like a small distance—just a temporary gap in the life they had built together. Little did she know, that week would be the turning point in her life.

The project wrapped up early—two days before it was supposed to—and Asmita, feeling the sudden urge to surprise Tapon, decided not to inform him of her early return. She had been looking forward to the look on his face when he saw her at home, waiting for him, ready to share her surprise.

Before she left for the project, they had hired a young woman to cook for them. A simple, sweet girl who had a warm smile and was a great cook. Asmita had communicated with her over WhatsApp a few times about cooking details, but it was nothing unusual—just the logistics of meal planning. Asmita hadn't even thought to tell the girl that she would be coming home early, and perhaps, unknowingly, left a door open for disaster.

When she landed early in the morning, the last thing on her mind was any kind of complication. She had her key in hand and opened the door as she always did, her heart racing with excitement to surprise Tapon.

But the sight that greeted her when she stepped into the apartment shattered everything she thought she knew.

There, on their shared bed, was Tapon with the cook, his arms wrapped around her. They were tangled in the sheets, unaware of Asmita's presence. For a long moment, Asmita stood frozen in the doorway, her mind struggling to process what her eyes were seeing.

The scene before her was nothing short of a nightmare. Tapon, the man she had trusted with her heart, the man she thought was her future, was in bed with someone else. The woman who had shared their space, their home, the one Asmita had trusted to help in the kitchen—she was in his arms.

Her breath caught in her throat, and instinctively, without thinking, Asmita grabbed her bag, her movements sharp and frantic. She didn't know what she was doing; she just needed to get away. She stormed out of the apartment, her mind whirling with shock and disbelief. The door slammed shut behind her, and the tears she had been holding back began to fall. But there was no time to process. No time to think. She needed to escape, and so, she dragged herself down to the street.

A taxi was parked by the curb, and Asmita, in a daze, hailed it with trembling hands.

"Where to?" the driver asked as she slid into the backseat, the door slamming shut behind her.

"I don't know," Asmita muttered, her voice barely audible. The driver glanced at her in the rearview mirror, sensing something was wrong.

"Everything okay?" he asked, his tone cautious but polite.

"No," Asmita snapped, her emotions spilling out uncontrollably. "Nothing is okay."

The driver hesitated, sensing the turmoil within her, but pressed on. "Well, I need you to know... you better find another taxi if you're in trouble. I don't want to get caught up in anything."

In a flash, anger surged through Asmita. She had just witnessed her entire life fall apart, and now this stranger was questioning her. She was beyond caring about anything at that point.

"Do you have any idea what I just walked in on?" she shouted, her voice thick with hurt. "I just found my boyfriend with my cook in our bed, after two years of thinking I had everything figured out! I trusted him, and I can't even—" Her voice broke, but she was determined to continue. "And now you're telling me to find another cab?

What would you do if this happened to you?"

The driver remained silent for a moment, his grip tightening on the steering wheel. After a few seconds, he started the engine and turned to face her briefly. "Look, I'm sorry, but you need to pull yourself together. You can't just let this consume you like this. You've got to deal with this, or you'll lose yourself."

Asmita, still trembling with shock and rage, said nothing. She simply stared out the window, the tears still streaming down her face, her mind lost in the chaos of what had just occurred.

Her phone buzzed in her hand, and through tear-filled eyes, she saw Sangeeta's name on the screen. She answered it quickly, her voice shaking as she greeted her friend.

"Sangeeta," Asmita said, barely holding it together, "I don't know what to do. Everything... it's all falling apart. I need to find a place to stay. Do you know of any guesthouses or hotels nearby? I just—"

"Asmita, what's going on?" Sangeeta's voice came through the phone, full of concern. "Why are you asking for a guesthouse? What happened?"

Through the lump in her throat, Asmita broke down, her emotions finally spilling over in a flood of sorrow. "Sangeeta, he... he was with her. With the cook. On our bed. I... I walked in on them. After everything... after thinking we were about to get married... he was with her."

Sangeeta was silent for a moment, taking in the weight of Asmita's words. Then, with a soft sigh, she spoke again, her voice full of empathy. "Asmita... I'm so sorry. I can't imagine what you're going through right now. But listen to me—don't stay there. I'll find you a guesthouse. It's the safest option. You can't go back there tonight."

Asmita nodded, though she knew Sangeeta couldn't see her. "I just need to get away, Sangeeta. I need space. Please."

"Don't worry," Sangeeta said softly. "I'll find you somewhere to stay. You don't need to be alone right now. Just take a breath, okay? I'm here for you."

After the call ended, Asmita wiped her eyes, the confusion and hurt still overwhelming. She had never felt more alone in her life. The person she thought she could trust had betrayed her, and the life she had built in her mind had crumbled in an instant.

The taxi driver glanced back at her. "Guesthouse?" he asked, his voice quiet, understanding that words weren't necessary anymore.

"Yes," Asmita said softly, her voice barely audible. "Just take me to the nearest guesthouse."

As the taxi pulled away, Asmita couldn't help but think that she was leaving behind more than just a home. She was leaving behind the life she thought she had, and stepping into an unknown future—one that she wasn't sure she was ready to face. But she had no choice. This was her reality now.

TWELVE

THE DESPERATE PLEA

Days passed, and the silence between Asmita and Tapon grew heavier. Asmita had shut herself off from him completely, unable to face the man who had betrayed her in such a painful, shocking way. Her phone remained silent when his name appeared on the screen, and when the calls kept coming, she couldn't bring herself to answer them. Each time, she simply let the ringing fade away into the distance.

It wasn't that she didn't care, or that she didn't feel the sting of the past. But the hurt was too deep, and the betrayal too raw. Asmita knew that there were no words that could undo what had happened. There were no apologies that would make the picture of Tapon in bed with someone else disappear. It was an image seared into her mind, one she couldn't escape no matter how hard she tried.

But Tapon didn't give up. Day after day, he called, his voice desperate, pleading for a chance to explain. He even tried calling from an unknown number, but still, Asmita didn't pick up. She couldn't. She wouldn't.

After several failed attempts to reach her, Tapon finally turned to Sangeeta. He called her one evening, his voice sounding frantic on the other end of the line.

"Sangeeta, please, can you tell me where Asmita is? I need to talk to her. I've been trying to reach her, but she won't answer my calls. Please, I need to see her. You have to understand," he pleaded, his voice almost breaking with emotion.

Sangeeta, who had been listening intently, didn't answer immediately. She had been trying to keep Asmita's pain at bay, offering her comfort and space, but hearing Tapon's desperation now only made her anger rise. She felt torn—part of her wanted to protect Asmita from further pain, but another part of her could sense the need for closure, for both of them to have their say.

"I can't tell you where she is," Sangeeta said, her voice firm. "She doesn't want to see you, Tapon. You've hurt her in a way that's beyond words, and right now, she needs time. She needs space to figure things out."

"I know I've messed up, Sangeeta," Tapon interrupted, his voice strained. "But I need to talk to her. She's not listening to me, and I need someone who can understand. You're her friend. You have to understand. Please, just tell me where she is. I can't take this anymore."

Sangeeta was silent for a moment, her mind racing. She knew what kind of man Tapon had been—charming, affectionate, but deeply flawed. He had made mistakes, and now he was trying to fix them, or at least, that's what he claimed.

Finally, after what seemed like an eternity of indecision, Sangeeta sighed. "Okay, fine. I'll meet you, but only because you're clearly desperate. We'll meet, but I'm not making any promises. You need to be honest with me, Tapon. I won't tolerate any more lies."

Tapon's voice changed in an instant, relief flooding through him. "Thank you, Sangeeta. I'll meet you wherever you want. I just need someone to listen to me. I need to explain. Please, just give me a chance."

Sangeeta thought for a moment, then nodded, even though Tapon couldn't see her. "Okay, let's meet at the secluded café near the park. It's quiet, and no one will bother us. 7 p.m. sharp."

The time for their meeting was set, and Tapon seemed almost too eager to agree.

When Sangeeta arrived at the café that evening, she found Tapon already seated at a corner table, his hands fidgeting nervously with the napkin in front of him. He looked different somehow—more haggard, more desperate—but still carrying that same charm that had once drawn Asmita in.

Sangeeta walked over to the table, her eyes cold and unwelcoming. She sat down, folding her arms across her chest as she regarded him silently for a few moments.

Tapon looked at her, his expression filled with both guilt and longing. "Thank you for agreeing to meet me," he said, his voice barely above a whisper. "I know I've messed everything up, but I just want a chance to explain myself."

Sangeeta didn't respond immediately. She simply stared at him, the anger and frustration she had been holding inside for so long beginning to surface. She wanted to say so many things—tell him how much he had hurt her best friend, how badly he had betrayed Asmita—but instead, she kept her mouth shut, waiting for him to speak.

Finally, Tapon exhaled sharply, as though the weight of his thoughts had been pressing down on him for too long. "It was a huge mistake, Sangeeta. I don't even know how it happened. Asmita was gone, and I was missing her so much... I don't know. I started drinking more than I should have, and then she—" His voice trailed off as he struggled to find the right words. "She was sweet. It just... happened. And now I feel like I've ruined everything."

Sangeeta's eyes narrowed, her voice rising with disbelief. "You're sitting here, telling me that you fucked your cook because you were missing Asmita? Because you were drinking and feeling lonely?" Her voice grew louder, the anger in her chest bubbling to the surface. "Tapon, are you seriously trying to justify this? You think that's an excuse?"

Tapon's face flushed with shame, but he continued to speak, as if he couldn't stop himself. "It wasn't like that! I didn't mean for it to happen. I swear, I thought about Asmita the whole time. It was like... I don't know... I wasn't in control. It was just one mistake, and I swear it won't happen again. I was out of my mind with the thought of her being gone."

Sangeeta slammed her hand on the table, unable to contain herself any longer. "You think this is just one mistake? You think this is something you can brush off? How dare you!" Her voice shook with the intensity of her anger. "You betrayed Asmita. You ruined everything, and you're sitting here trying to act like it was nothing more than a lapse in judgment? You have no idea what you've done to her, do you?"

Tapon opened his mouth to respond, but Sangeeta didn't let him speak. "No, Tapon. You don't deserve Asmita. You don't deserve someone like her who gave you everything. You're pathetic, and I'm glad she didn't have to see you for what you really are."

Tapon's eyes welled up, but the shame was too much for him to process. "I... I didn't know what else to do," he whispered, his voice trembling. "I just wanted to fix it all. I wanted to make it right."

Sangeeta stood up abruptly, her chair scraping harshly against the floor. She threw one last look at him, filled with a mix of anger, sadness, and pity. "There's nothing to fix here, Tapon. You broke it, and now you have to live with the consequences. You're not the person Asmita thought you were, and frankly, I'm glad she found out now rather than later."

With that, she turned and walked away, leaving Tapon alone at the table, his head bowed in defeat, the weight of his actions finally settling in.

THIRTEEN

Uncertainty in the Office

Asmita stepped into the office building, the familiar hum of the busy environment surrounding her as she made her way to the elevator. It had been two weeks since she had taken leave to deal with the emotional wreckage . The anxiety that had plagued her every day had finally pushed her to take time off, but now, returning to the office felt like a mountain she had to climb.

Her palms were clammy, and her stomach churned with nervousness. She hadn't prepared herself for what she might face today—her first day back after the sudden leave, with no explanation offered to her boss or colleagues. Asmita wasn't one to shy away from responsibility, but today, her usual confidence seemed to be slipping through her fingers like sand.

Her colleagues greeted her warmly as she walked past them, some with brief nods, others offering comforting smiles. "Glad to see you back, Asmi," one of them said, and another chimed in, "Don't worry about anything. It happens to all of us. Take it easy for a couple of days."

The reassurance from her peers helped, but the knot in her stomach remained. Asmita tried to shake off the feeling, reminding herself that she wasn't doing anything wrong. Still, her eyes kept darting to the door of her boss's office, and a sense of dread crept over her.

She had been at the company for a while now, known for her dedication and professionalism. But today, something about facing her boss felt different. Her heart raced as she imagined Mr. Saxena, her boss, reprimanding her for her sudden leave. She couldn't shake the fear of his disappointment, even though logically, she knew she had done nothing wrong. She had simply taken time to heal. But still, the fear lingered.

Asmita tried to visualize the scene: Mr. Saxena, tall and imposing, standing behind his desk, giving one of his speeches about the company's commitment to excellence. He would emphasize the need for each employee to put forth their best effort, reminding everyone that he was answerable to the board, and every decision he made was scrutinized.

Would he see her absence as a sign of weakness? Would he question her dedication to her work? She had no way of knowing. All she could do was replay these imagined scenarios in her mind, each one making her more anxious.

The thought even crossed her mind: What if this was it? What if her boss used this as an excuse to question her capability? Maybe this was the turning point where he would point out that she wasn't up to the job anymore. Would he dismiss her? The idea made her stomach flip. Was she ready to leave the job, to give up her career over something like this?

Shaking her head, she tried to push these thoughts away. She had no reason to think like that. But still, the anxiety refused to subside.

Finally, Asmita walked to Mr. Saxena's office, her heart pounding with every step. She knocked on the door, her hand trembling as she reached for the doorknob.

"Come in," Mr. Saxena's voice called out from inside.

She opened the door and stepped inside, trying to maintain a professional demeanor despite the whirlwind of emotions inside her. Mr. Saxena looked up from his desk and gave her a warm, somewhat surprised smile.

"Asmi," he said, his tone gentle. "It's good to see you back. Please, take a seat."

She sat down, the tension in her shoulders slightly easing at the sight of his calm, unthreatening expression.

He leaned forward slightly, his elbows resting on the desk. "How are you now?" he asked, his tone softening. "Are you feeling better? Is everything okay to resume your work?"

Asmita breathed a small sigh of relief. She had expected something harsher—an admonishment or some sort of reprimand—but instead, Mr. Saxena's concern was genuine. She hesitated, trying to collect her thoughts before responding.

"I'm better now," she said quietly, trying to hide the vulnerability in her voice. "I'll do whatever it takes to catch up on the work I missed. I can even do extra time if necessary."

Mr. Saxena nodded thoughtfully. "You don't need to do that, Asmi. I don't expect you to make up the time like that. You've been through something difficult, and your health is more important. In fact," he said, leaning back in his chair, "I noticed that you've been under quite a bit of stress recently. You look like you haven't slept for a couple of days. It's fine, though. You don't need to explain further if you don't want to."

Asmita's breath caught in her chest. How did he know? She hadn't mentioned anything to him, nor had she given any reason for her stress to be so obvious. Was it that apparent? She felt a wave of embarrassment wash over her.

He continued, "In your absence, Reshma took over your file. I think it would be wise for you to take her into your team for now, so you don't feel like you have to shoulder all the pressure. I know you've been managing a lot, and I don't want you to feel overwhelmed."

Asmita sat there in stunned silence. Reshma? Was he suggesting she needed help? Did he know something she didn't? How could he possibly know about her struggles? Did everyone in the office see through her?

As she sat there processing his words, a swirl of questions filled her mind: Why did I need Reshma to help me out? Does he know about my condition? Does everyone think that I'm not handling things well? Did he just hint at something bigger?

The room felt suffocating for a moment, and Asmita struggled to regain her composure. Was it possible that her boss had somehow learned about her emotional state without her saying anything? Was that why he had mentioned her lack of sleep? Or maybe it was just his experience as a manager, noticing the signs of stress in his employees.

Sangeeta's voice echoed in her mind: "Maybe you're overthinking things, Asmi." Could it be that she was just projecting her own fears onto the situation?

Mr. Saxena, noticing her silence, gave her a reassuring smile. "Don't overthink it. Just focus on getting back into the rhythm of things. You don't need to put too much pressure on yourself right now."

Asmita nodded slowly, the words sinking in. She had been so wrapped up in her anxiety that she hadn't stopped to consider that her boss might just be trying to help, not criticize her. She was relieved, but at the same time, a nagging sense of doubt lingered. Was it a sign of depression that I'm overthinking everything? she wondered.

As she left Mr. Saxena's office, her mind raced with thoughts she couldn't yet fully grasp. Am I really this fragile? Am I hiding something that's obvious to everyone around me? But no answers came. All she could do was walk back to her desk, feeling a little less burdened than before, but still uncertain about what the future held.

As she sat at her desk, Reshma came over to offer her a warm smile. "Hey, Asmi. Let's get started on the project, shall we?"

Asmita forced a smile, nodding. But the questions swirling in her mind only grew louder, and for the rest of the day, she couldn't shake the feeling that something deeper was at play—something she wasn't yet ready to face.

FOURTEEN

ASMI, WHY DIDN'T YOU FORGIVE HIM?

The evening was quiet, a comfortable hum in the background as Sangeeta and Asmita sat at the small dining table in Sangeeta's cozy apartment. The dim light of the pendant lamp above cast a soft glow over the table, highlighting the array of Chinese dishes Sangeeta had ordered. It was Asmita's favorite: Cantonese-style food, the delicate flavors of sweet and savory filling the air. Asmita couldn't help but smile at the familiar smell, momentarily forgetting the weight of her thoughts.

But as they ate, a sense of unease began to settle over Asmita. She was thankful for the meal, but Sangeeta's quiet demeanor hinted that there was something more on her mind. The two had been friends for years, and Sangeeta could read her like an open book. There was no hiding her feelings from her now, especially when she was trying so hard to hold it all together.

Suddenly, Sangeeta set her chopsticks down and looked across the table at Asmita. There was a glimmer of something serious in her eyes.

"Asmi," Sangeeta began, her voice gentle but with an edge of determination, "there's something I want to talk about. I know this isn't easy, but I think it might help you get to a place where you can truly heal. You've been through a lot, and you've been holding so much in." She paused, her gaze unwavering. "I want to ask you about Tapon."

Asmita's heart skipped a beat. The mention of Tapon, her first love, the man who had broken her heart, was still a raw wound. She tensed up, her chopsticks suddenly feeling too heavy in her hands. She swallowed, but the lump in her throat wouldn't go away. "What about him?" she asked, trying to keep her voice steady, though her emotions were already rising.

Sangeeta took a breath, leaning forward slightly. "I'm just wondering, Asmi, why didn't you forgive him? I mean, after everything that happened—after you walked in on him with your cook, after what he did to you—why didn't you forgive him? Everyone always said he was a great guy, a gem of a boy. What harm is there giving him another chance instead?"

Asmita felt a surge of emotion flood her chest. She had never expected Sangeeta to bring up Tapon in this way, and the sudden rush of anger and confusion overwhelmed her. She shot back before she could stop herself. "Would he have forgiven me if he had caught me in bed with another man in his bedroom?" Her voice was sharp, more defensive than she had intended, but the words tumbled out anyway.

Sangeeta blinked at the question, clearly taken aback. She didn't answer immediately but paused, considering Asmita's words. "I... I honestly don't know, Asmi," Sangeeta replied softly. "But maybe he should have. Maybe you both should have had a different kind of understanding, one that didn't involve betrayal."

The words lingered between them, and Sangeeta seemed to choose her next words carefully. "But you didn't forgive him, and I think that's something you need to confront. Maybe it's because you've always been too pure for today's world. Most men—and honestly, many women—are like that. Flawed. Weak. We all carry our flaws, and they show up in the worst ways. Tapon may have hurt you, but he's not the only one. People don't always live up to the standards we set for them."

Asmita's eyes filled with tears, but she blinked them away quickly. "I wanted to forgive him. I really did, Sangeeta. But I couldn't. I couldn't get past what I saw. How could I? After everything we had, to find him like that... it shattered me. I didn't want to be naive, to ignore the reality of what happened just because I loved him."

Sangeeta reached across the table and gently placed her hand on Asmita's. "I know, Asmi. I know. It's just hard to let go of someone you thought you would spend your life with. But the way he treated you was a betrayal. And sometimes, walking away is the only way to protect yourself."

Asmita nodded slowly, her breath shaky. "But if I had forgiven him... I don't know. Maybe things would have been different. Maybe I would have been able to move past it, but the image of them together... it still haunts me."

Sangeeta sighed and leaned back, her gaze softening. "But Asmi, you can't keep living in that moment. You can't keep carrying it with you, letting it define your life. You need to find a way to forgive yourself, to release that burden, even if you can't forgive him."

Asmita swallowed hard, her mind spinning with the idea of forgiveness—something she didn't even know she was capable of anymore. "I don't know how, Sangeeta. I really don't. He's the first person I ever loved, and now... now I feel like I don't even know who he really was."

Sangeeta's voice was gentle as she spoke again. "And that's exactly why you need to talk about it. Not just about Tapon, but about Subrato too. You need to confront these memories—the good and the bad. All of it. You can't keep running from these things, Asmi. They'll eat at you until you let them go."

Asmita looked up at Sangeeta, her heart heavy. "But what if the good memories outweigh the bad ones? What does that mean? Does that mean I should forgive them?"

Sangeeta shook her head, her expression serious. "It's not about whether the good memories outweigh the bad ones, Asmi. It's about understanding that the bad ones can't define you. You don't have to forgive them to move on, but you do need to acknowledge what they did and how it made you feel. You can't keep pretending it didn't hurt. You have to face the pain, so it doesn't continue to control you."

Asmita paused, her thoughts spinning. The idea of facing those memories, of confronting what had happened with both Tapon and Subrato, was daunting. She wasn't sure if she was ready to relive the past, to open those wounds again. But a part of her knew Sangeeta was right. She couldn't keep avoiding it. She couldn't keep burying her pain and pretending it didn't matter.

"I'll talk to Paromita," Asmita said, her voice steadying with resolve. "I'll tell her everything."

Sangeeta smiled softly, her eyes full of warmth and understanding. "You're stronger than you think, Asmi. This isn't about forgiving them—it's about forgiving yourself.

And that's where the healing begins."

As they finished their meal in a comfortable silence, Asmita felt a sense of clarity she hadn't expected. It wasn't about forgetting the past or erasing the hurt. It was about facing it head-on, understanding it, and letting it go. It would take time, but she was beginning to understand that facing her pain was the first step toward freeing herself from it.

The journey wouldn't be easy, but with Sangeeta's support, and Paromita's guidance, Asmita was starting to believe she could take that step. And for the first time in a long while, she felt ready to confront the past, no matter how painful it might be.

FIFTEEN

WHISPERS IN THE OFFICE

Asmita sat at her desk, staring at her computer screen, but her mind was elsewhere. The words on the page seemed to blur together, and the clicking of the keyboard felt distant. She had tried everything to stay alert—drinking water, taking short walks, even splashing cold water on her face in the bathroom. But no matter how hard she tried, the drowsiness kept creeping back in.

Her head felt heavy, as though a thick fog had settled inside it. The side effects of the sleep medication Dr. Paromita had prescribed were starting to take their toll. At first, Asmita had been grateful for the pills—anything to help her sleep, to make the exhaustion fade. But now, the medicine made her feel groggy and detached, like she was moving through the world in a haze. She had asked Dr. Paromita for help, but she hadn't expected to feel this "dumbed down" throughout the day, her thoughts sluggish and disjointed.

As the hours dragged on, she could feel her eyelids growing heavier, her focus wavering. She had barely slept the night before, lying awake in bed, her mind racing with thoughts of the past, of Tapon, of Subrato. And when sleep had finally come, it had been late—too late. She had woken up late again, rushed to get dressed, and skipped breakfast in her hurry to get to the office. The constant cycle of sleep deprivation and drowsiness was beginning to take a toll on her physical and mental health, and it was becoming harder to hide.

"Asmita?" Reshma's voice broke through her fog. "Are you okay? You've been looking out of it all day."

Asmita blinked, realizing she had been staring blankly at the screen for far too long. She forced a small smile, hoping it would mask the fatigue she felt. "Yeah, just tired," she said, her voice hoarse. "I'm fine. Just a little drowsy."

Reshma didn't look convinced. She leaned in closer, her voice lowering. "Are you on sleeping pills? Because you look like you're about to fall asleep at any moment."

Asmita hesitated. The truth felt like a weight she wasn't sure she wanted to carry. But with Reshma, she felt a strange sense of comfort, as though she could trust her. After all, Reshma had always been understanding and supportive. She had seen Asmita at her best and worst and hadn't judged her.

Asmita sighed, rubbing her forehead. "Yes, I'm on sleeping pills," she admitted quietly. "I've been seeing Dr. Paromita, a psychiatrist. She prescribed them to help me sleep better. But the side effects are... not great. I feel drowsy all the time now. It's making it hard to focus on work."

Reshma's eyes softened with concern. "I had a feeling something was off with you lately. You've been kind of out of it, even during meetings. But you're still here. That's the most important thing, right?"

Asmita smiled weakly, grateful for Reshma's words, but the weight of her exhaustion still hung over her. "I'm trying, Reshma. I really am. But it's hard. I'm not sleeping well, and when I do sleep, I wake up feeling like I've been hit by a truck."

There was a long pause before Reshma spoke again, her voice quieter now. "I don't mean to intrude, but... you've got Mr. Saxena asking around about you. He's been talking to people, even asking me about your progress. I think he has his suspicions about you—whether everything is okay or not. He's been asking if you're doing well. It's starting to feel like he's keeping tabs on you."

Asmita's stomach twisted at the thought of Mr. Saxena prying into her personal life. She had always respected him as her boss, but now, the idea of him scrutinizing her every move felt like an invasion. Her throat tightened, and she fought the surge of panic that threatened to rise.

"Mr. Saxena is being nosy about me?" Asmita asked, her voice laced with disbelief. "What does he think is wrong with me?"

Reshma shrugged. "I don't know. But he seems concerned. He asked me if I noticed anything odd about you lately, about how you've been feeling, if your performance is up to par. I didn't give him much, though. Just said you were fine, that you were handling your work like always."

Asmita swallowed hard, her mind spinning. "I don't need him prying into my business," she muttered under her breath. "I can't believe he's asking around. What if he finds out? What if he tells the board?"

Reshma lowered her voice even further, glancing around the office to ensure no one was listening. "Asmita, you can't keep this up forever. If he's asking, then maybe it's time you just told him. If you're struggling, you don't need to hide it from him. It's better to be honest than to have him start rumors about you."

Asmi's mind raced. Honest? Could she really tell him everything? Could she tell her boss that she was seeing a psychiatrist, that she was struggling with depression, that her life had fallen apart in ways no one could understand?

"I'm not sure I can just tell him, Reshma," Asmita said quietly, feeling the weight of her words. "I don't want him to think I'm incapable of doing my job. He might think I'm unfit to handle the pressure. I don't want to lose everything. I've worked too hard for this."

Reshma nodded sympathetically. "I get it. But you don't have to carry this burden alone. If you need to talk to him, just do it when you're ready. You shouldn't feel ashamed of getting help. It's not a weakness."

Asmita's thoughts began to swirl, the weight of the decision ahead of her pressing down on her shoulders. She had always prided herself on being strong, on being capable. But now, the pressure was too much. The constant exhaustion, the sleepless nights, and the never-ending anxiety were starting to feel like too much to bear.

Taking a deep breath, she looked up at Reshma. "You're right. Maybe I should talk to him. But not yet. I need a little more time to figure things out. I'm not ready to tell him everything, not yet."

Reshma gave a soft smile, a reassuring one. "Take your time, Asmi. But just remember—you don't have to face this alone. If you need help, I'm here. We all are."

Asmita smiled weakly, her heart heavy with the weight of everything she was carrying. She wasn't sure what the future would hold, but for the first time in a while, she felt like there was a glimmer of hope. She didn't have to carry the burden alone, and maybe, just maybe, she could take the first step toward healing—one conversation at a time.

As she sat back in her chair, her mind still spinning with thoughts, she realized that the road ahead would be difficult. But she would walk it, even if it meant facing her fears and confronting the pain she had been running from for so long.

SIXTEEN

I DON'T WANT TO FEEL LIKE THIS ANYMORE.

The small, peaceful waiting room in Dr. Paromita's office felt like a sanctuary compared to the storm swirling inside Asmita's mind. Her hands gripped the edge of the armchair as she tried to keep her composure, but the weight of everything—her exhaustion, her constant drowsiness, and the looming fears about her performance at work—felt almost too much to bear.

She had called Paromita on short notice, desperate for answers. Her work life was spiraling out of control, and the constant anxiety, coupled with the side effects of the medication, was making it impossible for her to focus. She needed guidance, and she needed it now.

As the receptionist ushered her into the chamber, Asmita felt a mix of relief and apprehension. The familiar scent of lavender and calming incense greeted her as she stepped into Dr. Paromita's office, which was warm and inviting. The soft beige walls and minimalist décor made the space feel comfortable, but today, Asmita couldn't seem to shake the tension in her chest.

"Asmita, it's good to see you," Paromita said, her voice gentle yet firm. "I'm glad you could make it. Please, sit down."

Asmita settled into the plush chair, but she couldn't quite get comfortable. Her hands were still shaking slightly, and the exhaustion from the past few days weighed heavily on her.

"I'm sorry to come in on such short notice," Asmita began, trying to steady her voice. "But I'm really struggling, Paromita. I've been feeling so drowsy all the time. I can barely stay awake during the day. It's like my mind is in a fog, and I can't focus at work. And then there's the office gossip—I can feel people talking about me, about how I'm 'not myself.' I'm afraid I'm losing control."

Paromita nodded, her expression understanding, though she was paying close attention to Asmita's every word. "I can see how overwhelming this must be for you, Asmita. It's not easy to manage everything when you're physically and emotionally drained."

Asmita swallowed hard, feeling the weight of her admission. "I'm really scared, Paromita. I just want to stop the medication. The pills you gave me—they're supposed to help me sleep, but they make me feel like I'm walking through life in a haze. I don't want to feel like this anymore. I want to be able to think clearly, to do my job, and not feel like I'm losing everything."

Paromita leaned forward slightly, her hands clasped together as she spoke in a calm, steady voice. "Asmita, I understand your concerns, and I know that the side effects of the medication can be difficult to handle. But let's take a step back and talk about why I prescribed those specific medications for you in the first place, and what the consequences of stopping them might be."

Asmita nodded, feeling a slight tension release as she realized that Paromita wasn't dismissing her concerns. She was being heard.

"I prescribed you a medication known as a sedative-hypnotic," Paromita continued. "This type of medication helps regulate your sleep cycle. It's crucial for treating sleep disorders and conditions related to anxiety, which we've discussed before. The medication helps to manage the neurological imbalance in your brain that's preventing you from getting restful sleep. Without that rest, your mind and body can't recover properly, which can worsen your emotional and mental state."

Asmita listened closely, but the worry was still there. "I know that the sleep has been an issue for me, but the drowsiness during the day... I feel like I'm not really here anymore. Like I'm detached from everything."

Paromita gave her a sympathetic look. "It's important to understand that the drowsiness you're experiencing is a side effect of the medication, but it's also a temporary one. The sedative-hypnotic medications I prescribed are designed to help you sleep at night, and their primary goal is to allow your body to rest and reset. However, since your sleep schedule is irregular and you've had trouble falling asleep at the right time, the timing of the medication can affect your daytime alertness."

As Asmita processed the information, she felt a slight sense of relief, but the fear still gnawed at her. "So, is there any way I can stop taking them? I don't want to feel like this anymore."

Paromita nodded. "I understand. But right now, stopping the medication would be premature and potentially harmful to your recovery. The issue isn't just sleep; it's the underlying condition—your depression and anxiety—that's causing your difficulty in managing your emotions and your stress. You're in a stage where therapy alone won't be sufficient, especially when you're struggling with sleep disturbances and physical exhaustion."

Asmita felt the weight of Paromita's words sink in. "So, the medication isn't just for sleep. It's for the depression, too?"

"Exactly," Paromita said softly. "Sleep disorders often go hand in hand with depression, and when you aren't able to sleep, your brain doesn't have the opportunity to repair itself. The medication I prescribed helps manage both the physical and emotional toll of depression by regulating your sleep, reducing anxiety, and promoting better cognitive function during the day. The fog you're feeling now is the result of your brain adjusting to the medication, and it will lessen as your body gets used to the dosage."

Asmita absorbed Paromita's explanation but still felt uneasy. "But what if I don't want to depend on these pills? I don't want to be someone who relies on medication just to feel normal."

Paromita's expression softened, her tone empathetic. "I hear you, Asmita. Many people feel the same way, but the key is that this is not permanent. You're not expected to stay on medication forever. The goal is to stabilize your condition and then gradually reduce the medication as your situation improves. Think of it as a crutch while you're healing. Once your depression is under control, once you're able to sleep properly and manage your anxiety, we can start tapering off the medication. But right now, it's important to follow the treatment plan to ensure that your condition doesn't worsen."

Asmita felt a flicker of hope, but the uncertainty was still there. "And what happens if I just stop taking them now? What would that do?"

Paromita sighed, her voice becoming more serious. "If you stop taking the medication abruptly, you could experience withdrawal symptoms. This might include increased anxiety, trouble concentrating, irritability, or even more severe sleep disturbances. Without the support of the medication, your depression could also worsen, and you might find it harder to function in your daily life. The medication is there to help you manage the immediate symptoms, and pulling away too soon could reverse the progress you've made."

Asmita felt a pang of frustration but nodded slowly, trying to accept that the road to recovery would take time. "So, what's the plan now?"

"I've already made some adjustments to your medication," Paromita said, looking at Asmita with a reassuring expression. "I've changed the timing of your dosage so that it works better for you in the evening. This should allow you to sleep more soundly at night and wake up feeling more refreshed. Over time, as we continue with therapy and the medication starts to take full effect, we'll gradually reduce your reliance on it. But for now, you need to stick with the plan. It's important for your long-term health."

Asmita sat back in her chair, her mind still spinning but with a clearer understanding of what was happening. She had been scared of becoming dependent on the medication, but now she saw that it was a temporary solution to a bigger problem. A necessary step in her healing process.

Paromita paused for a moment before continuing. "Let me explain in more detail the kind of medications I've prescribed for you. There are different classes of medications used to treat depression, and each works in a different way, depending on the symptoms and the underlying issues. The sedative-hypnotic you're on is just one piece of the puzzle."

She leaned forward, her voice becoming more informative as she began to break down the medication classes. "The most commonly prescribed medications for depression are called Selective Serotonin Reuptake Inhibitors (SSRIs). These work by increasing serotonin levels in your brain, which helps to regulate mood, anxiety, and stress. Serotonin is a neurotransmitter that plays a key role in happiness and well-being. SSRIs like fluoxetine (Prozac), sertraline (Zoloft), and escitalopram (Lexapro) are commonly used because they have fewer side effects compared to older medications. They help improve mood and energy, and they're often used to treat both depression and anxiety."

Asmita listened intently as Paromita continued, her explanation giving her a clearer picture of the landscape she was navigating. "Another class of medications, Serotonin-Norepinephrine Reuptake Inhibitors (SNRIs), like venlafaxine (Effexor) and duloxetine (Cymbalta), work similarly to SSRIs but also increase norepinephrine levels. Norepinephrine is another neurotransmitter that helps regulate mood and energy. SNRIs are often prescribed when SSRIs are not effective, especially for people who experience physical symptoms of depression like fatigue and body aches."

"Then there are the Tricyclic Antidepressants (TCAs) and Monoamine Oxidase Inhibitors (MAOIs)," Paromita continued, "but these are typically only prescribed when other medications haven't worked. They're older and tend to have more side effects. For example, TCAs like amitriptyline and nortriptyline affect serotonin, norepinephrine, and dopamine levels in the brain, but they can cause dry mouth, blurred vision, and dizziness. MAOIs, like phenelzine (Nardil), inhibit the enzyme that breaks down serotonin and dopamine, but they require strict dietary restrictions to avoid dangerous interactions with foods that contain tyramine."

Asmita absorbed the information, beginning to understand the complexities of her treatment. "So, the medication you've prescribed is part of a broader strategy to manage my depression and sleep issues?"

"Exactly," Paromita affirmed. "The goal of your treatment plan is to stabilize both your mood and your sleep. Right now, your depression is affecting your ability to sleep properly, and that, in turn, is affecting your ability to function during the day. We're using a combination of sleep aids and medications that regulate your mood and help you sleep, and this process will be gradual. The idea is to get you stable first, and then we'll work on reducing the medication as you improve."

Asmita nodded, feeling a sense of clarity she hadn't had before. She was starting to understand why the treatment was necessary and why the medication was part of the process. It wasn't just about the pills; it was about taking control of her health, one step at a time.

"You're doing great, Asmita," Paromita said with a reassuring smile. "Remember, this isn't a quick fix, but it is a path to healing. We'll take it one step at a time, and you're already making progress."

Asmita left the session feeling a little lighter, with a clearer sense of direction. The road ahead was still uncertain, but she felt more equipped to face it, understanding that healing wasn't just about therapy—it was about managing her mental and physical health, and taking the necessary steps to get better, one day at a time.

"Thank you, Paromita," she said quietly, her voice filled with a new sense of resolve. "I didn't understand all of this before. I think I can handle it now, knowing it's not forever."

Asmita left the session feeling a little lighter, with a clearer sense of what lay ahead. The path to healing would be difficult, but it was one she could walk—one step at a time, with the right support. And for the first time in a while, she felt like she was taking control of her own recovery.

SEVENTEEN

WHAT IF I FEEL IT TOO?

The clock ticked past midnight, the dim glow of the streetlights casting faint shadows across the room. Asmita lay awake, her mind restless, her body tense. Beside her, Sangeeta slept soundly, her breathing steady with the occasional soft snore. The sight of her friend—dressed in a revealing nighty that left little to the imagination—only added to Asmita's unease.

She turned her head slightly, watching Sangeeta's peaceful face. There was a time when Sangeeta's hugs had been her sanctuary, a safe harbor during turbulent days. But now, every touch felt loaded, every embrace lingered a second too long. Do I like it? The question gnawed at her. Or am I just too scared to admit that things have changed?

A quiet sigh escaped her lips. Maybe it was time they slept separately. Maybe boundaries needed to be redrawn before—

Just then, Sangeeta stirred. Her eyes fluttered open, dark and knowing in the dim light.

"Still awake?" she murmured, her voice thick with sleep.

Asmita stiffened. "Yeah. Just… can't sleep."

Sangeeta shifted closer, her fingers brushing against Asmita's arm. "Let me help you." Before Asmita could protest, a warm hand settled on her belly. The touch was gentle but deliberate, sending an unexpected jolt through her.

Her breath hitched. "Sangeeta—"

But Sangeeta wasn't stopping. Her hand slid upward, slow, testing. Asmita's pulse spiked.

"Stop." The word came out sharper than she intended. She sat up abruptly, heart pounding. "We're going too far."

Sangeeta's face fell. "Asmita, relax—"

"No. We need to talk about this." Her voice trembled. "If we don't, we'll end up in a messy breakup, and I—I don't want to lose you. You're too important to me."

Sangeeta's eyes glistened. "Then don't push me away. You were enjoying it too, weren't you?"

The accusation stung. "You're confusing things," Asmita shot back. "Maybe it's because of all your flings, all those casual relationships. You don't know the difference between love and—"

"I love you!" Sangeeta's cry was raw, desperate. Tears spilled over. "I'm not confused, Asmita. I've never been more sure of anything. This isn't about sex—it's about you."

The room felt too small, the air too thick. Asmita stood, pacing. "This isn't right. I should leave."

"No!" Sangeeta grabbed her wrist. "If you walk out now, I—I won't survive it. I swear, I won't." Her voice cracked. "At least stay in the same house. We'll sleep separately. Just… don't abandon me."

Asmita stared at her, torn between fear and guilt. The weight of Sangeeta's words, her tears, her need—it was suffocating.

But beneath it all, a terrifying question lingered: What if I feel it too?

The night stretched on, heavy with unspoken truths, neither of them sure where the lines were anymore.

The silence between them stretched, thick with tension. Sangeeta's grip on Asmita's wrist loosened, but her eyes remained locked onto hers, pleading.

Asmita swallowed hard, her voice barely above a whisper. "Sangeeta... you can't just say things like that. 'I won't survive it'? That's not fair."

"I know," Sangeeta admitted, wiping her tears with the back of her hand. "But it's the truth. You think I haven't tried to ignore this? To pretend it's just friendship?" She let out a shaky breath. "Every time I hug you, every time I hear you laugh—it hurts, Asmita. Because I want more. And I'm terrified of losing what we already have."

Asmita's chest tightened. "But what if I can't give you that? What if I don't feel the same way?"

Sangeeta's lips trembled. "Then tell me. Look me in the eye and say you've never once wondered. That you've never felt anything when I touch you."

Asmita hesitated. That was the problem—she had wondered. There had been moments—when Sangeeta held her a little too long, when their fingers brushed, when she caught her staring—that made her pulse quicken. But was that love? Or just confusion?

"It's not that simple," Asmita finally said, running a hand through her hair. "You're my best friend. My safe place. What if we ruin that?"

"What if we don't?" Sangeeta countered softly. "What if it's even better?"

Asmita shook her head. "And what happens when you get bored? When you realize this isn't one of your flings? I can't just—" She stopped herself, but it was too late.

Sangeeta flinched as if struck. "You really think that little of me?" Her voice was icy now. "That I don't know the difference between love and a fling? That I'd risk our friendship on a whim?"

Guilt twisted in Asmita's gut. "I didn't mean—"

"Yes, you did." Sangeeta sat up straighter, her tears drying into something fiercer. "You think because I've dated around, I don't know what real love is? Maybe I needed those flings to realize how different you are. How much you mean to me."

Asmita's breath caught. She had never seen Sangeeta like this—raw, vulnerable, yet so sure.

"I'm scared," Asmita admitted quietly.

Sangeeta's expression softened. "I know. So am I." She reached out, but this time, she didn't grab—just let her hand hover, waiting. "But we don't have to figure it all out tonight. Just... promise me you won't run. That we'll try to understand this."

Asmita stared at her outstretched hand. The weight of the moment pressed down on her—the fear of losing Sangeeta, the fear of crossing a line, the terrifying possibility that maybe, just maybe, she wanted to cross it too.

Finally, she exhaled. "Okay. We'll... talk. But separate rooms for now."

Sangeeta nodded, relief flickering in her eyes. "Okay. Thank you."

Asmita stood, her legs unsteady. But before she could leave, Sangeeta's voice stopped her.

"Asmita?"

She turned.

"Whatever happens... you're still my person."

Asmita's throat burned. She didn't trust herself to speak, so she just nodded and stepped out, closing the door behind her.

The house was silent, but her mind was louder than ever.

What if we're making a mistake?

What if we're not?

And beneath it all, the quietest, most dangerous thought of all:

What if I'm already falling?

EIGHTEEN

LETS GO TO PAROMITA

The café hummed with mid-afternoon lethargy, the clink of porcelain and murmur of conversations forming a protective bubble around their corner table. Dr. Paromita stirred her masala chai slowly, watching the cinnamon swirl into the froth as she waited for one of them to break the silence.

Asmita sat with her back to the wall, fingers clenched around a cooling latte. Sangeeta had chosen the seat facing the door—always restless, always ready to flee. The space between them might as well have been an ocean.

"So," Paromita finally said, setting down her spoon with deliberate care. "We're all aware this is... unconventional. Me knowing Sangeeta since college, you being my patient, Asmita. But since we're here—"

"She ambushed me." Asmita's voice was low but razor-sharp. "Literally pinned me down in bed after midnight with some... some teenage confession—"

"That's not what happened!" Sangeeta's cup rattled as she slammed it down. Several patrons glanced over.

Lowering her voice, she hissed, "I touched your stomach. Once. And you—"

"And then you pushed up—"

"Enough." Paromita's therapist voice cut through like a scalpel. "We're not here to litigate last night. We're here because you both want something from each other that isn't simple." She turned to Asmita. "You're shaking."

Asmita looked down at her trembling hands, surprised. "I haven't slept. My boss called HR this morning about my 'performance issues'. And now this?" A bitter laugh escaped her. "I can't lose my job over your... your epiphany, Sangeeta."

Sangeeta's face crumpled. "You think I'd ever let that happen? I'd quit myself before—"

"That's the problem!" Asmita's whisper was fierce. "You don't think. You just feel and expect everyone to keep up!"

A waiter approached nervously. Paromita ordered more chai without looking at him. When he fled, she leaned in. "Asmita. What do you need right now to feel safe?"

The question hung in the air like smoke.

"Time," Asmita said at last. "Space. To not have every fucking touch analyzed for hidden meanings."

Sangeeta made a wounded noise. "So that's it? Seven years of friendship just—"

"Did I say that?" Asmita snapped. "Christ, why does everything have to be all or nothing with you? Can't we just... pause?"

Paromita watched the understanding dawn on Sangeeta's face—the terrible, necessary realization that love sometimes meant stepping back.

The café's warm lighting did little to dispel the chill between them. Asmita stared into her latte, watching the foam dissolve—much like the careful boundaries she'd built over years of friendship. When she finally spoke, her voice was softer than before, frayed at the edges.

"It's not that I don't... feel anything." The admission cost her. "But when you touch me like that, I don't know if it's you I want, or just... not being alone."

Sangeeta's breath caught. A single tear splashed into her untouched espresso.

Paromita observed the shift, her therapist's mind noting the subtle changes: Asmita's white-knuckled grip easing slightly, Sangeeta's restless knee going still. "That's an important distinction," she murmured. "One worth examining. But not," she added firmly, "while you're sleep-deprived and facing HR meetings."

The rain outside intensified, matching the turmoil in the booth. Asmita traced the rim of her cup, her next words barely audible.

"I dream about you sometimes."

A stunned silence. Sangeeta's lips parted, but Paromita's subtle headshake stopped her.

"And how do those dreams make you feel?" Paromita asked.

"Terrified." Asmita laughed wetly. "Because when I wake up, I can't tell if it's wrong or just... too much."

Sangeeta reached across the table—then stopped, hand hovering. A question.

For the first time, Asmita didn't flinch away.

Paromita seized the opening. "Here's what we'll do. Asmita, you'll stay in the guest room until you find alternate housing. Sangeeta, you'll respect that boundary like your life depends on it." A meaningful pause. "Because someone's might."

She let that sink in before continuing, gentler now. "No more midnight confessions. No testing boundaries. If there's something real here, it'll survive some space."

Asmita exhaled shakily, her fingers brushing Sangeeta's still-waiting hand—just once—before retreating. "Okay."

"Okay," Sangeeta echoed, voice thick.

Outside, the rain slowed to a drizzle. Three women sat in the fragile peace of a ceasefire, each nursing their own private hope—and fear—of what might grow in this new, uncertain space between them.

NINETEEN

LOVE IS A
SLEEPLESS DRUG

The apartment was too quiet without Asmita's breathing beside her.

Sangeeta lay stiff on the bed, staring at the ceiling, the sheets tangled around her legs. Every rustle of the curtains, every creak of the floorboards felt amplified in the hollow dark. She turned to her side, instinctively reaching out—only to grasp empty space.

A sharp pang of loneliness twisted in her chest.

She sat up abruptly, rubbing her face. This is ridiculous, she told herself. You've slept alone before. But the thought rang hollow. The bed felt too big, the room too cold. Her pulse thrummed erratically, a drumbeat of something nameless and gnawing.

Fear. It struck her suddenly, a visceral dread that coiled around her ribs. What if Asmita never came back? What if this distance became permanent? The panic surged, her breaths turning shallow.

"Get a grip," she muttered, swinging her legs off the bed.

Her feet carried her to the kitchen on autopilot. The dim glow of the streetlights outside cast long shadows across the counter. Without thinking, she yanked open the liquor cabinet and pulled out a half-empty bottle of vodka.

The first gulp burned. The second went down smoother.

By the third, her limbs felt looser, the edges of her anxiety blurred. But the emptiness remained.

She stumbled back to bed, the alcohol buzzing in her veins, but sleep refused to come. The digital clock on the nightstand ticked from 1:15 to 1:47 to 2:03.

"Fuck this."

Before she could second-guess herself, she was padding down the hallway, her bare feet silent against the cold floor. She stopped outside Asmita's door—the guest room, she corrected bitterly—and hesitated.

Two knocks. Light, tentative.

No answer.

Another knock, harder this time.

"Sangeeta?" Asmita's voice was thick with sleep, laced with wariness. "What do you want?"

"I—" Her voice cracked. "I can't sleep. At all. I thought... maybe you could spare one of your pills? Just for tonight."

A beat of silence. Then, "You know I can't just give you my medication. We'd have to ask Paromita."

"Please." The word came out ragged. "Just one. I'm—I'm losing it, Asmita."

The door opened a fraction, and Asmita's sleepy face appeared—then her eyes widened. Sangeeta stood there in nothing but a thin camisole and shorts, her hair disheveled, her cheeks flushed from the vodka. The scent of alcohol wafted off her in waves.

"Oh my god," Asmita whispered. "You're drunk."

"Not enough," Sangeeta admitted hoarsely. "Not enough to stop feeling this."

Asmita's throat tightened. For a second, she just stared, torn between frustration and something dangerously close to pity. Then, with a resigned sigh, she grabbed her phone.

"I'm calling Paromita."

Paromita's voice was calm but firm through the speaker. "How much has she had to drink?"

"Enough that she's swaying," Asmita said, eyeing Sangeeta, who leaned against the doorframe like it was the only thing keeping her upright.

A pause. Then, "Give her one lorazepam. Just one. And make sure she drinks water."

"Are you sure?"

"It's either that or she ends up in the ER with alcohol poisoning and panic," Paromita said quietly. "One night won't kill her. But don't make a habit of this, Asmita."

Asmita handed Sangeeta the pill and a glass of water, her fingers brushing briefly against Sangeeta's clammy palm. "Here."

Sangeeta swallowed it without protest, her eyes glistening. "Thank you."

"Just... go to bed, Sangeeta."

But as Sangeeta turned to leave, something in Asmita's chest twisted. Before she could stop herself, she reached out and pulled Sangeeta into a quick, tight hug.

"You scared me," she murmured against Sangeeta's hair.

Sangeeta froze—then melted into the embrace for just a second before Asmita gently pushed her away.

"Goodnight," Asmita said softly, closing the door before either of them could say anything else.

Behind the door, Sangeeta stood still, the ghost of Asmita's arms around her, the pill and the vodka finally pulling her under.

TWENTY

SKIN AND SEDATIVES

Sangeeta woke to the sound of her own heartbeat—too loud, too fast—as if her body was punishing her for last night's sins. The digital clock on the nightstand blinked 12:37 PM in angry red numbers.

Noon. She'd slept through half the day.

She tried to sit up, but the room tilted violently. A wave of nausea rolled through her, and she clutched the sheets, waiting for the world to right itself. The pill had dragged her into a dreamless void, but now that she was awake, everything came rushing back:

The vodka bottle, slick with condensation in her trembling hands.

The way she'd pounded on Asmita's door like a woman possessed.

The look on Asmita's face—fear, exhaustion, something else she couldn't name.

And then, the hug.

Brief. Desperate. Over too soon.

Sangeeta groaned and buried her face in her hands. "God, what is wrong with me?"

Down the hall, Asmita had been awake for hours.

She sat on the edge of the guest bed, her phone heavy in her hand. Paromita's text glared up at her:

"We need to talk. Today."

No pleasantries. No room for argument.

Asmita exhaled sharply. She'd broken the rules last night—handing over medication, crossing a line she'd sworn to keep solid. But what was she supposed to do? Let Sangeeta spiral until she choked on her own panic?

Her fingers absently traced the edge of the blanket where Sangeeta had gripped it, her knuckles white with desperation. "You scared me," she'd whispered.

Had Sangeeta even heard her?

The apartment was too quiet.

Asmita moved through the kitchen like a ghost, the rhythmic *click-click* of the gas stove the only sound. She dropped sliced ginger into boiling water, the sharp scent cutting through the fog in her brain.

Habit. That's all this was. She'd made this tea for Sangeeta a hundred times before—after parties, after bad dates, after nights when neither of them could sleep.

The footsteps behind her were unsteady.

Asmita didn't turn around.

"I'm sorry," Sangeeta rasped.

The apology hung in the air between them, fragile as a soap bubble.

Asmita kept stirring. "You stink of vodka."

"I know."

A beat of silence. Then Asmita slammed the spoon down and shoved the mug across the counter. "Drink this. Then shower. You have an hour before Paromita gets here."

Sangeeta's fingers brushed hers as she took the mug. A spark. A flinch.

Neither of them acknowledged it.

Paromita arrived at exactly 2 PM, her therapist's mask firmly in place. She took one look at Sangeeta—pale, hollow-eyed, gripping her tea like a lifeline—and got straight to business.

"House rules," she said, pulling a notebook from her bag. "Starting today."

No alcohol in the apartment.

Sangeeta starts therapy with someone else.

No unannounced visits to each other's rooms. Text first.

Asmita nodded along, but her jaw was clenched so tight it ached. Temporary. This is all temporary.

Then Paromita turned to her, gaze sharp. "And you—stop policing her. You're not her keeper, Asmita."

The words landed like a slap.

Since when? she wanted to scream. Since when have I not been responsible for her?

But she stayed silent.

That night, Sangeeta lay awake again.

The apartment was too big, too quiet. She stared at the ceiling, counting the cracks in the plaster like they held the answers to questions she was too afraid to ask.

Next door, Asmita was probably asleep. Or maybe she was lying awake too, staring at the same damn ceiling.

Sangeeta rolled onto her side, pressing her palm flat against the wall that separated them. The plaster was cool under her skin, but she imagined she could feel warmth on the other side—the faint rhythm of Asmita's breath, the steady beat of her heart.

Pathetic.

But she didn't pull her hand away.

TWENTY-ONE

THE PERFORMANCE REVIEW

The fluorescent lights hummed overhead, casting a sterile glow on the HR waiting room. Asmita shifted uncomfortably in the cheap plastic chair, her eyes darting between the abstract paintings on the walls and the receptionist's immaculate nails clicking against the desk. She hadn't meant to come early, but now she found herself trapped in this awkward limbo, waiting for her performance review. The clock seemed to mock her, every second dragging on longer than the last.

Seventeen ceiling tiles. Asmita counted them again, her gaze drifting upward, though she could barely focus. She couldn't help it; her mind was scattered. How did she go from acing the quarterly presentation three months ago to this moment, unable to string a sentence together?

Her chest tightened with anxiety, and she leaned back in her chair, closing her eyes for a brief second, trying to calm the rising panic. Three months ago, she had been on top of the world—confident, clear, and respected by her colleagues. The numbers had been solid. The presentation had been flawless. But now, she felt like an imposter, a shell of the person she once was.

A cough from the receptionist snapped her back into the present. She smiled weakly, trying to appear composed, though her insides were a mess.

"Asmita Sen?" the receptionist called, her voice almost robotic.

With a deep breath, Asmita stood up and walked toward the door, her legs unsteady. Kapoor, the HR Manager, sat at the desk, his expression a mixture of calculated professionalism and veiled disappointment. He motioned for her to sit, and the moment she did, she was once again overwhelmed by the stifling atmosphere in the room.

Kapoor looked over her file, adjusting his glasses. "Asmita," he began, his tone polite but devoid of warmth, "let's get straight to the point. Your performance has been... concerning. You missed a few deadlines recently, and the quality of your work has significantly dropped."

Asmita felt her face flush. The words felt like knives, each one digging deeper into her sense of self-worth. She opened her mouth to respond, but her mind went blank.

"Three months ago, you were at the top of your game," Kapoor continued, giving her no time to process his words. "What happened?"

Asmita swallowed hard. She wanted to explain, to pour out the frustration and exhaustion she had been carrying for weeks now. The constant drowsiness, the medication, the emotional rollercoaster—but she couldn't find the words.

Kapoor, noticing her hesitation, leaned back in his chair, arms folded. "I have a suggestion," he said, his voice patronizing. "Have you tried yoga? Power poses? Maybe some vitamins could help clear that fog in your head."

Asmita blinked, struggling to hold back her frustration. Yoga? Power poses? She felt a wave of disbelief wash over her. Was this really how he was going to solve her problem? Was that really the advice an HR manager would offer to an employee dealing with a serious issue?

"I—I'm doing the best I can," Asmita finally managed to say, her voice wavering. "It's been... tough lately."

Kapoor sighed, clearly uninterested in her reasoning. "Well, I think it's time for you to step up, Asmita. This isn't how we expect our employees to perform. If this continues, you might not have a place here much longer."

Asmita's stomach twisted with dread. She had heard the warning in his tone.

Just as the weight of his words pressed down on her, there was a soft rustling from the corner of the room. Rahul, a junior colleague who had been in the office only for a year, stood awkwardly near the door, holding a file. He had overheard the tail end of the conversation. Asmita caught his eye, and for a split second, she saw something flicker in his expression—sympathy, maybe even understanding.

"Kapoor," Rahul said, clearing his throat, "I have the latest data analysis for you."

Kapoor waved him off dismissively, not looking up from his desk. "Leave it on the table."

As Rahul turned to leave, he paused for a moment, glancing back at Asmita. She met his gaze, her chest tight with anxiety. Before he could exit the room, he slipped a small card onto her desk. It was a therapist's card, simple and professional, but the gesture spoke volumes.

Asmita's heart skipped a beat. She reached for the card quickly, her fingers brushing against it, and tucked it into her pocket, feeling a strange sense of gratitude for this small act of kindness.

After Rahul left, Kapoor leaned forward, his eyes narrowing slightly. "I'll be blunt, Asmita," he said, "next month, we reevaluate your position. If you don't improve, we'll have to let you go."

Asmita could barely respond. Her thoughts were a blur, and the words felt distant, like they were coming from someone else. She had never felt so small, so incapable, and the pressure of it all was suffocating.

Before she could stand to leave, her phone buzzed. It was a message from Paromita: "Emergency. Sangeeta's missing."

Her heart skipped a beat, and her eyes widened in shock.

Kapoor looked at her curiously. "Everything okay?"

Asmita could barely process the question. "I—" She swallowed, struggling to find her voice. "I have to go. Something's happened."

She didn't wait for Kapoor's response. Asmita grabbed her things and rushed out of the office, her mind racing. Sangeeta was missing? What had happened? She couldn't comprehend it, but the urgency of the message drove her forward, away from the confines of the office and into a whirlwind of worry and fear.

The weight of the day's events seemed to fall away as she focused entirely on her phone, on the message, on finding Sangeeta. Whatever had happened in that meeting with Kapoor—whatever was being said about her performance—didn't matter right now. Sangeeta needed her.

And as she left the building, Asmita couldn't help but feel like she was on the brink of something bigger, something more significant than just a failed review. Something in her life was shifting, and she didn't know what the future held, but she was ready to face it, head-on.

TWENTY-TWO

THE SEARCH FOR SANGEETA

The city seemed alive with movement as Asmita left the office, but for her, everything felt still. Her mind was consumed by the urgent message from Paromita—Sangeeta was missing. The words echoed in her mind as she hurried down the street, her steps quickening with every second. What had happened? Where was she?

The weight of the day's earlier performance review still lingered, but it was suddenly irrelevant. The uncertainty about her job, her struggles with sleep, the mounting pressure—none of it mattered now. Sangeeta was missing, and that was all that mattered.

Asmita's phone buzzed in her hand, snapping her back to reality. It was Paromita.

"Asmita," Paromita's voice came through, urgent yet calm, "Sangeeta hasn't been at work today, and I can't reach her. She hasn't answered any of my calls either. I'm really worried. I think something's wrong. We need to find her."

Asmita's heart sank. "Where should we start looking? What should we do? I should have checked on her this morning. I shouldn't have just listened to her and gone to sleep without waiting for her to come back. "

"Meet me at my place," Paromita said quickly. "We'll go from there. I have a few ideas."

Asmita didn't need to be told twice. She barely remembered the drive across the city, her thoughts consumed by images of Sangeeta—her friend, her confidante—now out there somewhere, alone, maybe scared, and perhaps in trouble.

When Asmita arrived at Paromita's apartment, Paromita was waiting for her at the door, looking more composed than Asmita felt, but the worry in her eyes was evident.

"Sangeeta's been withdrawing for the past few days," Paromita said as she led Asmita into the apartment. "I thought it was just the stress of everything going on, but now I'm worried it's something more. She's always been a bit secretive, but this is different. She hasn't been answering my texts or calls."

Asmita sat down, trying to process everything. "Why wouldn't she tell us what's going on? Why would she just disappear like this?"

Paromita sighed, rubbing her temples. "I don't know. But I have a feeling something happened. Let's check her apartment. Maybe she's there. Maybe she just needed time alone, but—"

Asmita's phone buzzed again, interrupting the conversation. It was a message from Sangeeta, but it wasn't recent. Asmita read it aloud:

"I can't do this anymore. I need some space."

Her hands trembled as she finished reading, and Paromita's face hardened with concern. "That's not like her. If she needed space, she would have told me. This... this feels different."

"Let's go," Asmita said, standing up. The uncertainty was gnawing at her, and she had to do something. They couldn't just sit and wait for more signs. She grabbed her coat, and the two of them headed to Sangeeta's apartment.

When they arrived, they found the door locked, and Paromita retrieved the spare key from her bag. The moment they stepped inside, the atmosphere felt wrong. Sangeeta's apartment was usually a reflection of her—welcoming, vibrant, a sense of calm—but today, it was unsettlingly still.

They moved quietly through the apartment, checking the living room first. Nothing seemed out of place. The cushions on the couch were where Sangeeta usually left them, her books stacked neatly on the coffee table. But the air felt thick with something unspoken, a presence that was missing.

"I don't get it," Asmita murmured, moving toward the bedroom. "She always keeps her space organized. It doesn't make sense."

Paromita followed her, her eyes scanning the room. It was then that she noticed something: Sangeeta's phone was lying on the bed, face-up. The screen was locked, and no one had been around to see who had called or messaged her.

Asmita's heart began to race again. "She wouldn't leave her phone behind unless—"

"I don't think she meant to leave in a hurry," Paromita interrupted, her voice filled with unease. "Let's check outside. Maybe she went somewhere on foot."

They rushed to the building's front desk, asking the receptionist if she had seen Sangeeta leave or if anyone had visited her recently. The receptionist didn't have any useful information.

With nothing else to go on, they decided to widen their search. The café that Sangeeta frequented was just a few blocks away. It was quiet, a place where she would often go to gather her thoughts. As they walked there, Paromita spoke softly.

"I've been thinking about the text she sent me. 'I can't do this anymore.' Maybe it's something bigger than just work stress. Sangeeta's always been so strong, but something must have pushed her over the edge."

Asmita nodded, but her throat felt tight. She had always seen Sangeeta as someone who could handle anything, someone who was always there for others. To think that she was struggling so deeply, hiding it all—Asmita felt like she had failed her friend by not noticing sooner.

When they arrived at the café, the barista behind the counter greeted them warmly. "Hi, how can I help you?"

"We're looking for a friend," Paromita said, trying to keep her voice steady. "Her name is Sangeeta. Have you seen her today?"

The barista's face clouded with confusion. "Sangeeta? No, I haven't seen her today, but she was in here late last night."

Asmita's heart skipped a beat. "She came in late last night?"

The barista nodded. "Yeah, she was alone. She seemed a little distracted, you know? I offered to refill her drink, but she didn't stay long. She left in a hurry."

Asmita exchanged a look with Paromita. "Do you remember what time she left?"

The barista thought for a moment. "It was around midnight. I thought it was odd, but she seemed fine. She just wasn't her usual self."

"Thank you," Paromita said quickly, pulling Asmita away from the counter. They both stood there in silence for a moment, trying to make sense of what they'd just heard.

Late at night? Alone? Distracted? It didn't add up.

"Let's head to the park by the river," Paromita suggested, her voice trembling slightly. "Maybe she went there to think. It's a place she's gone when she needed space before."

The park wasn't far, and they hurried there, their footsteps echoing in the otherwise quiet streets. As they reached the entrance of the park, they saw a police officer standing by a small group of people. The officer looked up and immediately approached them.

"Are you looking for someone?" the officer asked.

"Yes," Paromita said, anxiety creeping into her voice. "We're looking for our friend. She went missing today. Her name is Sangeeta. Has anyone seen her?"

The officer's face softened. "We've found someone matching her description. She's by the river, near the footbridge. She's confused but safe. We're making sure she's okay."

Asmita's breath caught in her chest. "Is she... alright?"

"She's been acting a little disoriented," the officer replied, "but she's not in immediate danger. She asked for you."

Asmita's heart slammed against her chest. "She's okay?"

The officer nodded. "She'll be fine. We're just taking precautions."

As they followed the officer to the spot by the river, a wave of relief washed over Asmita, though it was tinged with concern. When they reached the riverbank, they saw Sangeeta sitting on a bench, staring out at the water. Her eyes looked distant, and she didn't seem to notice their approach until Paromita called her name softly.

"Sangeeta," Paromita said, kneeling down beside her. "We were worried. What happened?"

Sangeeta looked up, her face pale, her eyes red from crying. "I'm sorry. I didn't mean to scare you. I just... needed to get away. I couldn't face everything anymore. I didn't know where else to go."

Asmita sat down beside her, reaching out to gently take her hand. "You don't have to go through this alone, Sangeeta. We're here. We're always here."

Sangeeta looked at Asmita, her expression a mix of relief and sadness. "I just didn't want to burden anyone. But I can't keep running away from everything."

The three of them sat there in silence for a while, the cool breeze brushing past them as they watched the river flow. Sangeeta had found her way back, but the journey was far from over. They had a lot to talk about, but for now, all that mattered was that they had found each other. Together, they would figure out the way forward.

TWENTY-THREE
LIFE IS A MIRACLE

The Train Station – 5:03 AM

The station smelled of diesel and damp concrete. Asmita's backpack straps dug into her shoulders, heavy with the weight of haphazardly packed belongings—three wrinkled kurtas, her dog-eared copy of The God of Small Things, and the orange prescription bottle she'd grabbed in the dark. The label read Lorazepam, but the pills inside were older, leftovers from a different life.

"Platform 3," Sangeeta announced, materializing beside her with two steaming paper cups. "Chai. Extra ginger. For courage."

Asmita accepted the cup, letting the heat sear her fingertips. Real. This is real.

A train whistle pierced the air. Across the tracks, a hunched old woman fed pigeons from a rusted tiffin box, her movements rhythmic as a metronome. The birds swarmed her feet in a flurry of gray wings.

"We don't have tickets," Asmita murmured.

"We'll pay the fine." Sangeeta grinned, that reckless grin that used to make Asmita's stomach flip in college. "Or bribe the conductor. Your choice."

The loudspeaker crackled: "Mangalore Express now boarding."

Sangeeta's hand found hers—not tentative, not questioning, just there. A tether.

"Last chance to chicken out," she teased, but her grip tightened.

Asmita thought of their barren apartment, the HR termination letter still unopened on the kitchen counter. The way her psychiatrist's office always smelled like antiseptic and false hope.

She stepped forward.

The train doors hissed open like a sigh.

The stray dog trotted past them, tail wagging, and leapt onto the train first.

"Even he's got places to be," Sangeeta laughed, dragging Asmita aboard.

The Journey – 6:45 AM

Golden light bled through the grimy windows as the train sliced through countryside. Asmita pressed her forehead to the glass, watching the world blur—telephone wires dipping and rising like musical staves, a lone cyclist wobbling along a dirt path, his shadow stretching long behind him.

Sangeeta sprawled across the seat, boots propped on the opposite bench. "Remember that field trip to Jaipur? When you got food poisoning and puked in the Taj Mahal's fountain?"

"You promised never to bring that up again."

"I lied." She tossed a peanut at Asmita's head. "You were magnificent. Like a tiny, furious volcano."

The memory warmed Asmita's chest. They'd been nineteen, invincible, drunk on cheap rum and the certainty that life would happen to them, not at them.

A vendor passed by hawking coconut water. Sangeeta flagged him down, bargaining with the ease of someone who'd grown up in bazaars. Asmita studied the way her hands moved—the silver ring she always wore on her thumb, the faded henna stains from a wedding they'd crashed weeks ago.

"Here." Sangeeta handed her a coconut, its top lopped off with a machete. "Drink. It'll cure your existential dread."

"That's not a medically recognized treatment."

"Neither are those." She nodded at Asmita's backpack where the pills rattled.

The sweetness of the coconut water surprised her. It tasted like childhood vacations, like before.

A commotion erupted further down the carriage—a group of college students singing off-key Bollywood songs, their laughter raucous and unselfconscious. One boy caught Asmita staring and winked.

"We could be them," Sangeeta said softly. "If we'd chosen differently."

Asmita thought of the alternate universe where she'd never slid into depression, where Sangeeta hadn't drowned herself in vodka and strangers' beds.

"Do you regret it?" she asked. "Us?"

Sangeeta's smile faltered. Outside, the landscape shifted—the first glimpse of the sea, a shimmering blue promise.

"Not yet," she said, just as the train plunged into a tunnel, swallowing them whole in darkness.

The Beach Town – 2:18 PM

The shack was smaller than it looked in photos, its tin roof patched with rust and hope. The landlord, a woman who introduced herself only as "Ammu—like the god, not the snack," led them inside with a hurricane lamp.

"No AC. No fridge. Toilet is out back," she said, thumping the wall. A gecko scuttled away. "But the view? Priceless."

She wasn't wrong. Through the crooked window, the Arabian Sea stretched endlessly, its surface dappled with sunlight like scattered coins.

Sangeeta flopped onto the lone bed, sending up a cloud of dust. "Home sweet hovel."

Asmita set her bag down carefully, her fingers brushing something tucked beneath the pillow—a dried frangipani flower, brittle with age.

"Previous tenant left in a hurry," Ammu said, catching her glance. "Like you two."

There was no accusation in her tone, only knowing.

"How much?" Asmita asked, changing the subject.

"For you?" Ammu's eyes flicked to Sangeeta's scarred wrists, then away. "Four hundred a day. Meals extra."

They paid in advance.

As Ammu left, she paused at the door. "The turtle nests hatch at moonrise. If you're lucky, you'll see life begin again."

The First Night – 9:32 PM

The candle guttered between them, casting monstrous shadows on the walls. Somewhere in the darkness, a coconut thudded to the ground.

"Truth or dare," Sangeeta said suddenly.

"We're thirty, not thirteen."

"Truth, then." She peeled a mango with her teeth, juice glistening on her chin. "When did you first think about dying?"

The question shouldn't have shocked her—not after everything—but Asmita's breath still hitched. The sea whispered against the shore, a relentless hush.

"The night my father called me a burden." The words crawled up her throat like insects. "After my diagnosis. He said... it was contagious. That I'd ruin my sister's marriage prospects."

Sangeeta's knife stilled on the mango peel.

"Your turn," Asmita forced out. "Why the scars?"

"Because the vodka wasn't cutting deep enough." A shrug. "Literally."

The candlelight caught the tears she wasn't shedding.

Later—much later—when the stars wheeled overhead and the candle drowned in its own wax, Sangeeta whispered:

"I don't want to be a tragedy anymore."

Asmita reached for her in the dark.

Their fingers tangled, salt-sticky and sure, as the first turtle hatchlings scrambled toward the sea.

The Hatchlings – 5:17 AM

Dawn came softly, the sky bleeding from indigo to the pale gold of a healing bruise. Asmita sat cross-legged in the sand, her cotton nightdress damp with sea spray, watching the turtle hatchlings scramble toward the water.

They moved with desperate, instinctive grace—tiny flippers paddling at the sand, their shells no bigger than her palm. Most wouldn't survive. Crabs, gulls, the merciless tug of the tide would claim them. But here, now, they fought.

"They're so fucking small," Sangeeta murmured beside her, voice rough with sleep.

Asmita didn't answer. Her throat ached. She thought of the pills in her backpack, the ones she'd promised not to take unless the darkness came crawling back.

A hatchling veered off course, circling blindly toward the dunes.

"Shit." Sangeeta scrambled forward, gently corralling it with her hands. "Wrong way, idiot."

The tiny turtle batted at her fingers before righting itself and joining the others.

Sangeeta's laughter was startled, bright. "Did you see that? It swore at me."

The sun crested the horizon, setting the sea on fire.

Asmita reached for Sangeeta's hand.

The Fisherman – 9:42 AM

The market smelled of salt and ripe fruit, of fish scales glittering like discarded jewelry underfoot. Asmita trailed after Sangeeta, watching as she haggled for lychees with a vendor whose teeth were stained red from betel nut.

"For you, pretty girl, half price," the man leered, tapping Sangeeta's wrist.

She recoiled, the scar tissue there pink in the sunlight.

Before Asmita could intervene, a voice cut through the crowd:

"Leave them be, Ramesh."

The fisherman was older, his skin leathery from decades of sun, his eyes the same startling green as the sea at midday. He tossed a coin at the vendor and handed Sangeeta the lychees. "Tourists shouldn't eat that trash anyway. Come. I'll show you real food."

His boat was a weather-beaten thing named Lakshmi's Revenge.

"You're not from here," he observed as they boarded.

"What gave it away?" Sangeeta grinned. "The city-girl stench?"

"The way you walk." He started the engine. "Like the ground might swallow you whole."

Asmita gripped the railing as they lurched forward.

The fisherman's grin was all gaps and gold. "Today, ladies, you learn how to live."

The Storm – 3:08 PM

The clouds rolled in fast—great, bruise-colored things that swallowed the sun whole.

"Monsoon's early," the fisherman grunted, turning the boat toward shore.

The waves grew teeth. The Lakshmi's Revenge bucked beneath them, wood groaning. Sangeeta whooped, arms spread like she could take flight, while Asmita clung to the mast, her stomach in her throat.

"You're enjoying this?" she shouted over the wind.

"Isn't this why we came?" Sangeeta laughed, seawater in her teeth. "To feel something?"

The first raindrops hit like bullets.

By the time they made shore, they were drenched, the lychees lost to the sea, the fisherman cursing in a language Asmita didn't know.

Sangeeta pressed her forehead to Asmita's, their breath mingling, their hands tangled in each other's clothes.

"Alive," she whispered. "We're alive."

The shack's roof leaked. They spent the evening catching rainwater in cooking pots, their laughter echoing off the walls.

Epilogue: Understanding Depression: A Journey Through Time

As we close the pages of *Am I Depressed?*, we are left with not only the story of Asmita's personal journey but also the lingering question: What is depression? And how do we understand it in the context of our ever-evolving world?

Depression is often misunderstood, reduced to a mere feeling of sadness or exhaustion. But the reality is far more complex. It is an illness, a mental health condition that can affect anyone, regardless of their background, age, or experiences. It is not a sign of weakness or a character flaw; it is an illness that, like any other physical ailment, requires understanding, treatment, and compassion.

The History of Depression

The history of depression stretches back thousands of years, but its understanding has evolved considerably. Ancient civilizations had various interpretations of what we now recognize as depression. In ancient Greece, it was called "melancholia," and philosophers like Hippocrates believed it was caused by an imbalance of bodily fluids. For centuries, the condition was linked to the humors of the body, a theory that dominated medical thinking well into the 17th century.

In the 19th century, the concept of "depression" started to take on a more recognizable form. Psychiatrist Emil Kraepelin, in the late 1800s, categorized what we now know as "manic-depressive illness" (bipolar disorder) and later, what we identify today as major depressive disorder. This marked a turning point in understanding depression as a distinct condition, separate from other mental illnesses.

Understanding Depression in the Modern Era

Today, we know that depression is a multifaceted disorder, often described as a persistent feeling of sadness, loss of interest, or inability to experience pleasure in life. It affects millions of people worldwide, transcending cultural, racial, and socio-economic boundaries. What we understand now is that depression can be triggered by a combination of genetic, biological, environmental, and psychological factors.

While the precise causes of depression are still being studied, advancements in neuroscience have given us much-needed insight into the brain's role. Depression is linked to chemical imbalances in the brain, particularly involving neurotransmitters such as serotonin, dopamine, and norepinephrine, which regulate mood, energy, and emotions. Brain imaging studies have also shown changes in areas of the brain responsible for emotions, memory, and decision-making in people suffering from depression.

Advances in Treatment

The treatment of depression has come a long way since the days of bloodletting and religious rituals. In the early 20th century, the use of psychoanalysis by Sigmund Freud and his followers sought to understand the unconscious mind's role in mental health. While psychoanalysis has become less dominant in the treatment of depression, it laid the foundation for modern psychotherapy techniques.

Today, treatment for depression is multifaceted. Psychotherapy, particularly cognitive-behavioral therapy (CBT), helps individuals recognize and change negative thought patterns that contribute to their depression. Medications, such as antidepressants, play an essential role in managing the condition by addressing the chemical imbalances in the brain. Selective serotonin reuptake inhibitors (SSRIs) and serotonin-norepinephrine reuptake inhibitors (SNRIs) are among the most commonly prescribed medications, helping to regulate mood and reduce symptoms.

In recent years, new and innovative treatments have emerged. One promising development is transcranial magnetic stimulation (TMS), which uses magnetic fields to stimulate areas of the brain associated with mood regulation. Another treatment, electroconvulsive therapy (ECT), though often misunderstood, is still used in severe cases where other treatments have failed. It has shown remarkable success in helping individuals who have not responded to traditional antidepressants.

The advent of personalized medicine is also making a significant impact. Genetic research is slowly revealing which individuals may respond better to certain types of antidepressants, helping to reduce trial and error in finding the right treatment.

Depression vs. Schizophrenia and Other Mental Illnesses

It's important to understand that depression, while deeply impactful, is distinct from other mental health conditions, such as schizophrenia. Schizophrenia, for example, is a severe and chronic mental illness that affects an individual's perception of reality, often leading to hallucinations, delusions, and disorganized thinking. Unlike depression, which primarily affects mood and motivation, schizophrenia can lead to significant cognitive impairment and an inability to function in day-to-day life.

Other mental illnesses, such as bipolar disorder, anxiety disorders, and personality disorders, have different manifestations and require different approaches to treatment. While depression can sometimes co-occur with other mental health conditions, it should not be equated with them. The treatment protocols and therapies that work for one condition may not necessarily work for another.

What sets depression apart is its accessibility and relatability. While it may feel isolating, depression is one of the most common mental health conditions, affecting over 300 million people globally. Yet, despite its prevalence, it often remains misunderstood and underappreciated. The stigma that surrounds mental illness still prevents many from seeking help, but the more we understand depression, the more we can remove that stigma and offer people the support and resources they need to heal.

As we look ahead, the future of depression treatment holds even more promise. Ongoing research into the genetic and neurological underpinnings of depression may one day lead to more targeted and effective treatments. There is hope that new therapies, including psychedelic-assisted therapy and neurostimulation, will continue to push the boundaries of what is possible for those suffering from depression.

While there is still much work to be done, the progress we have made in understanding and treating depression over the past century is remarkable. We have moved from viewing mental illness as a taboo subject to a more open and supportive dialogue. We now have tools that allow individuals to manage their depression and lead fulfilling lives.

Am I Depressed? is not just the story of one woman's journey through the depths of despair. It's a reflection of the millions of individuals who face the same questions every day. It is a reminder that depression is a real illness, but it is also treatable. It is not a life sentence. With the right support, treatment, and understanding, recovery is possible.

Life is not always easy, and depression can feel like a never-ending battle. But the more we talk about it, the more we educate ourselves and others, the more we understand the complexity of mental health, the more we take away the power of stigma. For those struggling with depression, there is no shame in seeking help. It is the first step in understanding that there is life beyond the darkness—life that is worth living. And sometimes, it's in the darkest moments that we begin to find our light.